"You little fool—
you absolute idiot!"

Crawford's voice rose in anger as he continued. "Why the hell couldn't you tell me what things were like at home? Are you so pigheaded, so full of pride, that you'd rather kill yourself than let anyone give you a helping hand?"

"Teddy and I can manage quite well without your interference," Gerry flashed back, her temper getting out of hand. "Anyway, you're always snapping at me. You can't blame me if I decided you'd be the last person I'd come to!"

She knew she sounded ungrateful for his kindness and couldn't understand why she felt like crying.

"Someone has to help you, Geraldine," he said softly. Her heart set up a rapid tumbling motion when Crawford leaned forward and placed his warm mouth against her own....

Pride's
Master

by

JESSICA STEELE

Harlequin Books

TORONTO • LONDON • NEW YORK • AMSTERDAM
SYDNEY • HAMBURG • PARIS • STOCKHOLM

Original hardcover edition published in 1979
by Mills & Boon Limited
ISBN 0-373-02309-X

Harlequin edition published January 1980

Printed in U.S.A.

CHAPTER ONE

GERRY BARTON breathed a sigh of relief that her usual parking spot was still free. They had a car park at Arrowsmiths where she worked, but come five o'clock with everyone trying to get out at the same time, she saved precious minutes by leaving her car the few hundred yards' walk away from the office. Checking her appearance in the rear view mirror, she noted with satisfaction that her dark brown hair was neatly in place in the tidy bun she wore it in for her place of business, and stepped out of her vehicle prepared to show anyone who might be interested the cool unruffled front she had adopted since she had come to work at Arrowsmith Electronics.

For once she was dead on time. She hated being late for work, but regretfully, it was often ten or fifteen minutes past the hour before she pushed her way through the swing doors of the company. Fortunately the twins had behaved themselves this morning and her sister Teddy had been all smiles when she'd left. Even so, she'd felt bound to ask, 'Are you sure you'll be all right?' Teddy had told her she was an old fusspot, for all, like the babies, they were twins themselves and Teddy was the same twenty-four years old as herself.

Basil Dyer fell into step with her as she turned the corner with Arrowsmith Electronics in sight. 'Good morning, Geraldine,' he greeted her. He was a middle-aged man, much married with a clutch of children he was said to adore, and was one of the few people at Arrowsmiths who hadn't been put off by the cool exterior she chose to show.

'Good morning, Basil. Family all right?'

'In rude health, you might say.' Gerry allowed herself a smile as his infectious grin beamed her way. Then he was serious. 'Wonder what today will hold—— Can do without any more drama like we had yesterday!'

'Drama?' Gerry wasn't with him, but showed only polite surprise. She had gone home early yesterday. Teddy had a dental appointment and there had been no one to look after the twelve-month-old Emma and Sarah. If anything dramatic had happened at the office yesterday it must have happened after she had left, because everything had been drearily mundane when she'd left.

'Don't tell me you don't know about Cyril Gillett?—I thought he was your boss.'

Basil had her full attention now. She had been working for Mr Gillett for fifteen months now and any drama concerning him concerned her too.

'I had part of the afternoon off yesterday—Mr Gillett wasn't taken ill, was he?' He'd been all right when she'd left, but now she came to think of it, he had been looking rather strained just lately.

'I expect he's feeling a bit sick this morning,' Basil said, looking not at all put out at the thought. 'He got the push yesterday.'

'Push?' Gerry's footsteps faltered and Basil slowed down to her pace. 'You mean he got the sack?' and at Basil's confirming nod, Gerry schooled her features to hide the disquiet of her feelings. Though it took a tremendous effort, because you couldn't see a person for some part of most working days without some sort of feeling coming through. 'W-what happened?'

'It's only rumour so far,' Basil seemed to be trying to look as though he hated to be the one to impart the news, but it was common knowledge that he and Cyril Gillett had never hit it off. 'But as far as I can make out, the boss man himself came down from London and without waiting to go to the office that's usually reserved for him, he went straight into Gillett's office and within an hour Gillett was leaving the building with his briefcase bulging with the personal impedimenta he'd collected over the years.'

They reached the swing doors and Basil stood back and Gerry waited inside the roomy foyer for him to join her inside. There were other workers making their way to their offices and by unspoken mutual consent, she and Basil took the stairs, neither wanting their conversation to be overheard in the crowded compartment of the lift.

'You mean Crawford Arrowsmith himself came down?' She had never seen him herself, but knew of his visits because she had often typed out the notes Mr Gillett took with him into the Board meetings Crawford Arrowsmith chaired.

'He did. Now if that doesn't signify that something big has gone wrong I'll eat my Sunday hat!'

Gerry had to agree with him. It was well known by those nearest to the top executives that while keeping a finger on the pulse of the running of the Layton branch, Crawford Arrowsmith preferred the heads of departments to make their own decisions. They came to the door of her office, Basil's office being some yards further down the corridor.

'Don't know what you'll be doing today, but word has it the big man intends to stay around for a few days, so you'll soon know something, I expect.'

With his words ringing ominously in her ears, Gerry went into the office that was hers and closed the door behind her, and sure she wasn't being observed, leaned weakly against it, taking her mind back over her conversation with Basil Dyer. She still couldn't believe it—couldn't—and not wanting to believe it she stared at the open door between her office and Mr Gillett's, and felt the compulsion

to check his office for herself. Surely Basil had got it all
wrong.

Mr Gillett's office was larger than her own. She had
been in it many times, but whereas before his desk had
always been liberally strewn with papers, when she walked
slowly through the open door, it was to observe that the
top of the desk was completely clear, and no sign of Mr
Gillett. Her heart set up a rapid beat as the truth of what
Basil had said sank in. Even so she just had to pull open
a couple of drawers in the desk for further confirmation.

'Looking for something?'

The cool, icy tones struck her ears, causing her to give a
guilty start. Never before had she looked into Mr Gillett's
private drawers, and she felt like a criminal caught red-
handed as she looked up in the direction of the voice.

She had to look up a long way to the speaker, who she
saw was an athletic-looking, dark-haired man somewhere in
his thirties. Even while she was instructing herself to stay
cool—closing the drawers with as casual an air as she could
muster, unhurriedly straightening up to her five feet seven
inches—the dark-haired man left his position by the door
and came to look down his straight nose through the hardest slate grey eyes she had ever seen.

She didn't want this cold-looking individual to be Crawford Arrowsmith, but felt in her bones he could be no other
as he pinned her with a calculating look that told her he
was nobody's fool. She felt the hairs on the back of her
neck prickle and wanted badly to flee for cover, for all she
had done nothing wrong. But the image she had managed
to put over and maintain during the last fifteen months,
though wobbly at that moment, was not going to desert
her now, she decided.

'I haven't lost anything,' she was proud of the way she
managed to hold his chilling look. 'This is Mr Gillett's
office.' It still was until she was told differently. 'I think

perhaps you may be the one who has lost something—
your way, perhaps?'

She could find no reason for the antagonism she felt
for this man. But it was instant, and for the life of her she
couldn't back down. Though if she had thought to disconcert him by her cool manner—as had happened with
a good few before him—then she was very much mistaken,
for apart from a slight narrowing of his eyes, not in any
degree a shade warmer, she could see no reaction at all.

'So good of you to come to the office on time—I take it I
am speaking with Miss Geraldine Barton?'

Obviously word had got to him about her tardy time
keeping—equally obvious was the fact that he hadn't heard
she always made up the lost time in her lunch hour.

'Yes, I'm Geraldine Barton,' she confirmed, ignoring his
sarcasm. 'I'm afraid you have the advantage over me ...
Might I be permitted to know who you are?' She mar-
velled at her own temerity—he had boss written all over
him, apart from the fact that his well-cut expensive grey
suit hadn't been made within thirty miles of Layton.

'Crawford Arrowsmith,' he said, by way of putting the
record straight, even though she had a feeling he knew all
the time she was aware who he was. 'You appear to be redundant, Miss Barton.'

If he wanted to shock her into dropping her pose he very
nearly succeeded. She half turned away from him so he
shouldn't see her face. She badly needed this job—it was
the best paid job to be had in Layton with her qualifica-
tions. And even with the high salary that went with being
P.A. to the Company Secretary, she and Teddy were hard
pushed to find the rent for the cottage. To find herself out
of a job, even if she managed to get another job that didn't
pay as well straight away, would cripple their finances.
With difficulty, she managed to school her features into the
calm she dared not let go, but could do nothing about
the pallor of her skin as she faced him.

'Do sit down before you fall down, Miss Barton.' His voice came through the rigid control she was exerting on herself. 'You're a big girl to have to scrape up off the carpet.'

That brought her to her senses quicker than any sal volatile could have done. She was tall, agreed, if five feet seven could be called tall, but was without any fat whatsoever on her bones. Indeed the constant worries over the last fifteen months—worry over Teddy's inability to cope now that Mark was dead, and the constant trying to make ends meet—had whittled her already slender frame down to a fragile slimness.

She felt herself being pushed down into the chair that only yesterday Mr Gillett had occupied, and followed Crawford Arrowsmith with her eyes as he walked over to the window. He had his back to her, and if she didn't know better she would have thought he was giving her these few minutes to get herself under control. But she doubted a man of his sort would have the sensitivity to care sufficiently how one of his underlings was feeling.

He turned suddenly, and she was made sharply aware of his eyes on her. She forced herself to sit up straight, masking the disquiet of her feelings as he came to stand over her.

'How much do you know of Gillett's handling of the company's affairs?' His question was short and to the point, his eyes refusing to let her look away.

'Quite a lot, I should think,' she came back, wondering if she was digging her own grave with that statement. Though if she was being made redundant as he had said, she had nothing to lose. She tried to shut out thoughts of Teddy, of beautiful Emma and Sarah, and concentrated on answering any questions Crawford Arrowsmith intended to fire at her as honestly as she could.

'You handled all his correspondence?'

'Yes.'

'All of it?'

He was being persistent, she thought. 'Yes—as far as I know.'

'As far as you know?' His tone was hard; he should have been a barrister—he'd make any witness in the box quake at the knees, she thought, as he barked the question at her.

'Well ...' she hesitated.

'Well?'

She had no intention of being disloyal to Mr Gillett. It was just that when she was late in, very often Mr Gillett had opened the post himself. But since Crawford Arrowsmith already knew about her bad time-keeping—though nothing would drag from her the reason for it—and since she was being made redundant anyway, she might just as well own up now, she thought with a fatalistic 'I've got nothing to lose'.

'Occasionally I arrive ten or fifteen minutes late.' A couple of times it had been as much as half an hour, but she wasn't about to sink herself without trace—he would never understand anyway. 'On the mornings I'm late Mr Gillett was good enough to start on the post for me.'

'Was?' he picked up. 'You said "was". Have you been in touch with Gillett since you left here yesterday?'

They didn't come any sharper than Crawford Arrowsmith, she thought, biting hard on a hasty retort that would have blown her cool image. 'I met one of the other office staff as I came in,' she told him. Basil wouldn't thank her for mentioning his name. 'He said there'd been a spot of bother after I had left yesterday.'

'Did your informant also tell you Gillett had been dismissed?'

So it was true. Even while she was wondering what Mr Gillett had done to warrant instant dismissal, her interrogator was asking if she knew why the Company's Secretary's services had been dispensed with, and when she said, 'No,' he was insisting:

'You're sure you have no idea?'

Crawford Arrowsmith was treating her as if she was a criminal—as if whatever it was Mr Gillett had done wrong, she had been party to it. To have her integrity questioned was something Gerry wouldn't lie down for, whatever the consequences.

'What is this?' she snapped hotly, her calm flying in all directions as she jerked to her feet, her eyes meeting his in a blaze of sparks that fairly flew from her dark brown eyes. 'If you're accusing me of doing something wrong, I demand to know what it is.'

For a moment he seemed arrested by the sudden beauty of her as Gerry forgot herself long enough to reveal a warmth hidden deep inside of her. Then his eyes frosted over.

'You demand, do you?—Would you mind telling me by what right you feel I should not be allowed to question someone who worked closely with a man I had thought was one of my most trusted employees—but was a man who turned out to be a cheat and a thief?'

At his harshly delivered words, the heat left her. Ridiculous though it might seem, she had the oddest notion that this hard man standing in front of her had been thoroughly sickened by the whole business.

'I didn't know,' she said quietly, trying to drag the remnants of her calm together. 'I . . .' The question had to be asked, but she was so afraid of the answer—Mr Gillett had been secretive about some of his work, but who would believe she hadn't known what was going on? 'Are you saying you think I was in league with Mr Gillett in his dishonesty?' She looked Crawford Arrowsmith directly in the eyes as she asked her question, and refused to look away even when it seemed his eyes would bore into the very soul of her.

After what seemed like minutes, but was in all probability only seconds, he told her, 'It had crossed my mind, I admit—but since you didn't always open the post, and it seems likely that the fraud was perpetrated through the post, I'm forced to give you the benefit of the doubt.'

Gerry looked away. It wasn't very satisfactory. She felt there was still some doubt clinging to her good name, but she had no way in which she could prove her entire innocence. People would think she had been up to her ears in cahoots with Mr Gillett, especially when she left—despite her reason for leaving being called redundancy.

Feeling physically sick, and unable to bear being in the same room with this hard, cold man any longer, she stepped round the desk and walked steadily back to the office next door. Once there she began emptying the drawers of the one or two personal items she in turn had collected during her time at Arrowsmith Electronics.

She had her dictionary, a spare pair of tights and her calculator assembled with various other pieces on the top of her desk when she became aware that Crawford Arrowsmith had followed her and was watching what she was doing. Tears came to the backs of her eyes and she desperately wanted to cry, but she wouldn't give him the satisfaction of seeing her break down. There would be no chance of giving way when she got home either—all her strength would be needed to bolster Teddy up when she told her the news; Teddy had been so happy when she'd left home this morning. She closed a drawer and turned her mind determinedly away from thoughts of Teddy. The most important thing at the moment was to get away from the head of Arrowsmiths without breaking down.

'Would you mind telling me what you're doing?'

His words reached her, quietly spoken, but with an

authority that demanded an answer. A semblance of control she had thought lost for ever came to her aid. 'I was under the impression I was leaving—— You did say I was redundant.' Pride was rearing up inside her, and she was just about to add that nothing would induce her to stay on a minute longer when he broke in:

'Redundant from being P.A. to Gillett—but I'm sure we can find you a job somewhere in the organisation.'

Relief that she hadn't told him what to do with his job flooded through her. She wouldn't have to go home and tell Teddy that she had no idea where the next month's rent was coming from. Still, the question was forced from her.

'You've said you'll find me another job—yet you still doubt my honesty?' Oh, if only she wasn't in a position where she had to accept his offer! It upset her greatly that she had to keep on working for him with him giving her honesty the benefit of the doubt.

'Your eyes tell me you've never done a dishonest deed in your life,' he surprised her by saying. Then any wonder she was left feeling at that remark disappeared as he walked to the door that led into the corridor, saying, 'I shall of course expect you to be here at nine sharp every morning —perhaps it might be an idea to curtail your love life.'

Gerry was glad the door was closed and she had the office to herself. Had he stayed another second she had an idea she would have hurled something at him. It was important to her that no one at Arrowsmiths see beneath the calm exterior, though she recalled she had been quite heated with him earlier, so he must know she was far from the cool being she would prefer him to think she was. Still, with a bit of luck he would be gone in a few days, and since on his subsequent visits he wasn't likely to bother with lesser mortals, she had probably seen the first and last of him. Her mind drifted on to what job he would find for her—and to the more worrying thought, would it pay as much as she was receiving now?

Since work still had to go on with or without the presence of a Company Secretary, Gerry knuckled down. She was familiar enough with the work to deal with routine matters, but anything she was unsure about she put to one side. She would know soon enough when she would be required to quit her office—until then, she'd work to leave it as clear as possible.

Basil Dyer poked his head round her door shortly after eleven. 'The rumours were right, then,' he said, coming in and closing the door. 'Mr Gillett's been thrown out on his ear.'

Basil probably knew far more about it than she did, so it was useless to attempt to cover up for Mr Gillett. The news of his dismissal would be buzzing all round the building by now.

'I'm still not sure what he did,' she confessed. Crawford Arrowsmith had said something about fraud, but that was as much as she knew.

'Apparently, so the story goes,' Basil qualified, 'old Gillett has been putting work out to tender and making sure his pals got the order.' Gerry had no idea how such a fraud could be worked other than that Crawford Arrowsmith had said something about it being worked through the post, and the puzzlement she was feeling showed in her face. 'It's easily done,' Basil went on to explain. 'All you need is to have a P.A. who doesn't get in on time to open the post.' Gerry gave an inward groan—did everybody know about her bad time-keeping? 'When the tenders came in all Gillett had to do was to ignore the lower tenders—regardless of their merit—accept the tenders from his cronies, and receive a nice fat rake-off.'

'You mean ...'

'I mean,' Basil put in as Gerry seemed incapable of continuing, 'that our erstwhile Company Secretary must have salted away thousands this past year alone.'

'And he was able to ... do this because I wasn't always

here to open his mail?' Gerry gasped, all pretence of being the cool efficient P.A. gone by the board at Basil's mention of the enormous amount of money involved. She was glad she was sitting down—she doubted her legs would have held her.

'Strewth, it's not all down to you, you idiot,' Basil looked down at her kindly. 'It helped him, I suppose—but I imagine he had some correspondence addressed to him personally?' Gerry nodded dumbly. 'There you are then—I expect those would be the higher priced tenders. For all we know, though, they might not even have come through the mail—he could have had them delivered to his home and brought them in with him.'

As Basil went on talking in the same vein, Gerry began to feel better, but only slightly. She wouldn't, she knew, be able to lose this feeling of guilt in a hurry. It seemed to her that, however indirectly, she was in part responsible for Arrowsmith Electronics being defrauded out of thousands of pounds. Perhaps Crawford Arrowsmith even thought she should have been more alert to what had been going on.

'Don't worry about it,' Basil could see how hard she was taking it, and was trying in his own way to comfort her. 'Mr Arrowsmith is loaded—I don't suppose he'll miss a few thousand.'

'Is he going to prosecute, do you know?' For all the wrong Mr Gillett had done, she couldn't bear to think of him being taken to court. He could even go to jail, she realised.

'Shouldn't think so—Mr Arrowsmith isn't a vindictive man. He would have been as mad as hell, of course, to have his trust broken, but since he's taken the action of chucking Gillett out—and let's face it, he couldn't very well keep him on after what he's done—he's got to have a man he can trust in that position—I expect he'll let it go at that.'

Basil went on to tell her whom they were tipping to take

Mr Gillett's place. It seemed there were three men in the running as far as office gossip went, but the general opinion was that Crawford Arrowsmith would not drag his feet over appointing the new man. Basil said nothing about her role as P.A. to the new Company Secretary, so word couldn't have got out yet that she was being found another position in the firm. Her pride prevented her from acquainting him with this piece of news. She liked Basil, he was a pretty uncomplicated sort of person, but she knew once she'd disclosed that piece of information it would be all over the building in half an hour.

'Well, I'd better go and do a bit more,' Basil said at last. 'With Mr Arrowsmith in the building, I'd better make it look as if I work here.'

He brought the smile, faint though it was, he had been hoping for from Gerry. It was well known that Basil Dyer worked harder than most.

Gerry had enough work to keep her busy that day. Teddy phoned during the afternoon as she often did. Gerry knew how lonely her sister felt—at home with the twins while she was away at work all day. Teddy seemed to have lost the art of mixing with people since her husband Mark had died, whereas before she had always been the life and soul of any party. Gerry spent some minutes in talking to her sister, assuring her she would leave the office at five sharp and be home before she knew it.

She had been expecting all day for Crawford Arrowsmith to send someone with instructions on which department she was to move into—he wouldn't come and see her himself, of that she was sure—and as the hands of the clock neared five to five, she began gathering her things together. At one minute to five she put the cover on her typewriter and stood up. She hated clock-watching like this, but Teddy was going through a bad patch—rather a long bad patch, admittedly—and she needed the security of having her at home. The minute hand ticked over to the hour and she picked up her bag. At the same time the handle on the outside door turned, and as she paused, hoping against hope, the door was pushed open and she looked up to see Crawford Arrowsmith standing there.

Her spirits plummeted—no chance of leaving on time now. Teddy would be anxiously watching the clock at the other end, but there was absolutely nothing she could do about it if she wanted to be kept on at Arrowsmiths, and she desperately needed this job.

'Still here?'

Sarcastic brute. 'I don't usually leave until five,' she told him, glad to find herself outwardly cool and calm at least.

'Yesterday must have been an exception.'

Of course he would have expected her to be at her desk when he'd called to see Mr Gillett yesterday; trust him to comment on her absence. She didn't answer him. It was nothing to do with him that Teddy had had to go to the dentist yesterday. Mr Gillett had been in his employ then, and he had not questioned her need to have time off. All the same, she couldn't help feeling uncomfortable as Crawford Arrowsmith stood there, obviously waiting for her to say something. He looked so sure of himself, so totally in charge as his eyes flicked from her face to her figure and back again, that she would have dearly loved to say something to jolt him.

'Have you decided which department I shall be working in?' she found herself asking while trying to get a look at the clock. He had walked further into the room and the clock was partly hidden by his shoulder.

'I shan't keep you many minutes,' he said coolly, without turning round, seeming to know why her eyes were straying over his shoulder. 'I'm sure your date will think you're worth waiting for.'

Their eyes locked, his definitely challenging, hers refusing to back down and enter into any discussion with him that wasn't about business. She had a feeling he was trying to draw her out, trying to get her to lose her calm air. But she refused to lose any of her outward cool, though inwardly she felt herself quivering with an unidentified feeling of alarm. It was almost as if her guardian angel was warning her to take care—this man was different from any other man she knew and could verbally annihilate her if she made one false move. Then suddenly some of her tension lifted and she had a feeling she had imagined he was trying to get a rise out of her, for he was saying:

'I haven't yet made up my mind what to do with you. For the time being you can report here at nine every morning.'

There had been a slight emphasis on the word *nine* that wasn't lost on her. 'Very well,' her tones were as cool as his. 'Though I don't know what I shall occupy myself with.' She had spent today clearing up. It was going to be a long day tomorrow with nothing to do.

'I shouldn't worry about that, Miss Barton—I'm sure we'll be able to keep you busy.'

It seemed he had nothing further to say to her—she daren't look at the clock again, didn't want to let herself in for another jibe about her date thinking she was worth waiting for—if he only knew, she hadn't been out on a date for more than a year. She picked up the handbag she had deposited back on the desk when he had come in, and was surprised when he went to the door and held it open for her. She halted briefly as she reached him and felt an unaccustomed jolt in the region of her stomach at his closeness when his voice arrested her.

'Until tomorrow, Miss Barton,' he said in cool, sardonic tones, his words sounding ominous in her ears—it was almost as if he was threatening her.

'Goodnight, Mr Arrowsmith,' she replied equally coolly.

As she raced to where she had parked her car, the uneasy feeling being in his presence aroused in her quickly vanished as she put him to the back of her mind. She was being ridiculous—over-anxious because she fully expected to find a tearful Teddy waiting for her when she got home; she had imagined all sorts of nuances in his voice that hadn't been there. His 'Until tomorrow' meant that, and no more. Since he had decided he would be the one to tell her what she would be doing each day until he had decided what to do with her, he had meant purely and simply that he would see her and give her her instructions for the day.

She pushed Crawford Arrowsmith out of her mind as she tried to get more speed out of the A35 than it wanted to do, and headed the car in the direction of the cottage she shared with her sister and the twins in the village of Little Layton on the outskirts of town.

Teddy was watching in the window when she pulled her ancient car round on to the patch that did service for a drive—one day they would get round to having it concreted, but for the moment there were other calls on their money.

'I thought you were never coming,' Teddy greeted her when she went in.

'Sorry, love—one or two changes at the office today and I was caught just as I was leaving.'

They were very close, though not identical twins, Teddy being blonde in contrast to Gerry's dark brown hair, and as children they had shared each other's emotional pains. Gerry hadn't meant to tell Teddy anything of what had happened today; Teddy was insecure enough without having to experience the sinking feeling she had felt when she'd thought she was going to have to leave Arrowsmiths.

Fortunately Teddy didn't enquire into what changes had taken place, but went on to tell Gerry some of the trauma involved in keeping a pair of one-year-old twins out of mischief throughout the day. 'What with Emma pulling over the clothes horse, and Sarah trying to eat her shoes, I'm absolutely whacked,' Teddy ended.

'Never mind, Ted, I'm here now. You put your feet up —I'll see to them for a while.'

Gerry went over to the playpen where the incorrigible pair were happily engaged in slinging building blocks at each other, and knelt down to say hello to them. Instantly two pairs of arms were raised aloft, one dark-haired twin like herself, and one a blonde like Teddy. In no time she had one apiece straddled over each hip, mindless of the fact she would have to get the iron out when they were tucked up in bed and press her suit.

This was the time she enjoyed best—the time when she was at home with these two scamps. Not for the first time she came to wonder if she was really cut out for the commercial world. She had worked hard to get her D.P.A., and to hold down the job of P.A. to a Company Secretary should have been sufficient for her. Her mind dwelt briefly on Robin Preston—if things had been different she might now be married to Robin, and since Teddy and she were twins, and Teddy had given birth to twins, she herself might well by now have babies of her own to love and care for.

Hurriedly she snatched her thoughts away from private yearnings. She was being disloyal to Teddy. Teddy hadn't asked her to give up Robin—Teddy had no idea Robin had even asked her to marry him.

CHAPTER TWO

By the skin of her teeth, Gerry made it to the office with one minute to spare the next day. She had been up half the night with Sarah, and since she hadn't wanted Emma to wake up and start crying in sympathy, it had meant taking

Sarah downstairs and walking up and down with her for what seemed like hours on end, for every time she stood still to rock her, Sarah sent up a whimper of protest.

Before she opened her door to begin work she knew she would be glad when five o'clock came round. Inside her own office she glanced at the clock, saw it was dead on nine, and thought, 'How's that, Mr High and Mighty Arrowsmith?' and leaned against the door, putting a slender hand in front of her mouth as she gave way to a delicious yawn.

'I see you didn't take my advice.'

The voice coming from the other room, startling when she had thought herself to be alone, had her jerking upright and away from the door. She looked through the dividing door into the room that had been Mr Gillett's. There, leaning negligently back in his chair, the desk before him housing a pile of papers that told her he must have been hard at it for at least an hour, sat Crawford Arrowsmith. As though compelled Gerry was drawn to step towards that door, stopping at the threshold between the two offices.

'Advice?' she queried, striving for her practised unflappable front. It would never do for him to see how easily he could disconcert her.

'I advised you to curtail your love life,' he said with cool insolence, and without waiting for any sort of answer to that, went on, 'Late nights don't suit you, Miss Barton.' His tone was cold, causing her to wonder if he really meant her to feel the wreck she must so obviously look. 'Or is it the effort of getting to your place of business at the appointed time that has you yawning even before you start your day?'

She knew for certain he was trying to get a rise out of her, but if he was waiting to see the sparks fly out of her eyes as he had done yesterday when she had momentarily lost control, he was in for a very long wait.

'You're wrong,' she said, marvelling that her words sounded so cool when she was so churned up inside.

'On which count?'

'I'm sorry?' She feigned not to know what he was talking about.

'Are you telling me it isn't your love life that makes you all bleary-eyed in the morning—or that you didn't get up extra early to be here on time?'

'My love life is no concern of yours.' She wondered how she dared to say that as she saw his lips tighten at her detached tone. 'And since I have every intention of being here on the stroke of nine in future,' she hoped she was going to be able to stick to that, 'I see no point in this catechism.'

'You cheeky ...' he stopped. She knew he had bitten off something very uncomplimentary, then was staggered to see the tight line of his lips disappear and what could pass for a smile cross his mouth. He couldn't be admiring her stand against him, she knew that, and for one awful moment she had a dreadful feeling he was going to dismiss her on the spot. She waited with tension mounting for the ace she was suddenly convinced he had up his sleeve. 'Since you and I will be working closely together for some time, I shall be able to see for myself what time you arrive *and depart*, won't I?' he said, with a return to the coolness he had shown earlier.

'Working together?' The cloak of calmness she had adopted since she'd seen him sitting there threatened to fly away from her. She took a deep breath, striving to bring its escaping folds closer around her.

'The whole set-up of this office needs looking into.' His eyes were boring into her, threatening to break her composure at any second. 'I have decided before I can hand over the reins of Company Secretary to anyone, the whole running of this section needs looking into—I shall do the job myself.'

Gerry took hold of herself as his words sank in. She didn't want him telling her again to 'Sit down, Miss Barton, before you fall down'. She moistened suddenly dry lips and cursed herself for that dead giveaway of her nervousness.

'Er—is it likely to take long—I mean, how long will you be here?'

The smile she had thought had been hovering broke through, revealing perfect strong white teeth. Fascinated for a moment, she stared at his mouth. It was a warm mouth when he smiled, she thought absently, until she discerned that there was no humour in his smile, just pure satisfaction that he had all but unseated her calm.

'I'll be here for as long as it takes, Miss Barton—for as long as it takes.'

Then there was no time for her to have any clear thoughts on what he had just told her. The feeling of disquiet that she was going to have to put up with him—not only put up with him, but see him daily since it appeared he was going to work from Mr Gillett's office for an indefinite period—had to be brushed aside, as Crawford Arrowsmith got straight down to issuing instructions for what he wanted her to do that day.

By mid-morning she was forced to give way to the reluctant admiration that had started to grow once he'd got started. One couldn't but admire the way the smallest detail was checked, the largest, most complicated of issues dealt with in a thorough and concise way. Nothing it seemed was overlooked by his eagle eye, and where Mr Gillett would sometimes dump a file in his pending tray saying, 'We'll look at that tomorrow,' there was none of that with Crawford Arrowsmith.

'What's this lot?' he asked at one stage, taking a batch of files from a cabinet Mr Gillett had always kept locked.

Gerry had to confess she didn't know. 'There were certain things Mr Gillett said were confidential to the board room only—I never handled anything from that cabinet.'

His face set in stony lines, his lips tightening as he flipped through every one of the files. She wondered if he believed her when she told him she had no idea what the files contained, and stood ready to defend herself if he challenged her statement. Then he looked across at her, his eyes fastening on her, taking in the tenseness about her. She saw his mouth relax, saw again the warmth of his mouth and steadied herself ready for more of his stinging sarcasm. But when he spoke, his voice was devoid of sarcasm—instead she thought it was touched with a superior type of amusement, and she didn't care for that either.

'Don't tie yourself up in knots, Miss Barton—I'm sure you're a regular little George Washington.' Then, waiting only briefly to see if her composure would crack, he went on, 'I think it's about time you were let into one or two secrets of confidential board room matters.'

And while it was sinking in that unbelievably Crawford Arrowsmith believed her, trusted her, he was getting down to the business of telling her what he wanted doing with this file—dictating several letters in connection with the next file—and without any break in his concentration, he worked solidly through file after file.

By the time lunch time came around Gerry's head was spinning. She wondered if he intended to break for lunch, for it seemed he was oblivious of the time. But at ten past one he called a halt and finished the letter he was dictating to lean back in his chair and flick his eyes over her.

She was conscious that a strand of hair had worked its way loose from the severe knot at the back of her head. It bent its way into a wave to caress the side of her face, the end still confined by pins. She knew it would soften the whole effect of her cool, calm image, but couldn't allow herself the weakening movement of pulling it back into place. Crawford Arrowsmith would know for sure he had disconcerted her if she did that.

'I bet you're quite something when you decide to let yourself go,' he said, his eyes holding hers to catch her start of surprise at his personal comment.

'You're never likely to know, are you?' she came back after a couple of seconds of marshalling her cool. She didn't like at all the way that ghost of a smile flickered over his mouth, and wished she'd remained quiet. She hadn't intended any hint of challenge in her words, but thought he might construe them that way—though it was hardly likely that the head of the Arrowsmith empire would look twice at her; not that she wanted him to, of course. It was with the utmost relief she saw he was going to ignore her remark, though she couldn't help feeling slightly uncomfortable as he ignored it, for all her comment had been deserved.

'We'll break for lunch now—I expect you'll be going along to the canteen. The worst of the queue will be over by now.'

Gerry returned to her desk hoping he would be going out soon. For economy reasons she always brought a sandwich to the office. The canteen meals were subsidised by Arrowsmiths, and were inexpensive, but even so with her small appetite it still worked out cheaper to bring a sandwich for lunch, besides which by cooking at night she was always sure Teddy had one good meal a day.

She fiddled around for five minutes, but when Crawford Arrowsmith showed no signs of leaving the office, she was forced to pick up her bag and step out into the corridor outside. Teddy had asked her to get some teething gel for Sarah anyway, so she'd go and get that first and then go back and eat her sandwich.

In ten minutes she was back, noting with satisfaction that the door between the two offices was closed. Good, he'd gone out—she could eat her sandwich in peace. After demolishing her sandwich, she delved into her bag and applied a smear of lipstick. She wore very few cosmetics, being fortunate enough to have a clear creamy skin that didn't require the expense of artificial aids.

With twenty-five minutes of her lunch hour gone, she flipped through the shorthand she had taken down earlier. If he wanted that lot doing before she went home—apart from anything else he had lined up for her this afternoon —she reckoned she'd have no time to lose if she was to leave on the dot of five that evening.

Popping out briefly to wash her hands and secure that strand of waving hair so that it should not work loose again, she returned to her desk and within five minutes was fitting stationery and the correct number of carbons into her machine. She was a good typist and unerringly her fingers beat out a steady rhythm on the keys. When the door of the connecting office opened she was so startled she hit three keys in rapid succession and they knotted together in her machine.

Her fingers strayed to the edge of her desk. 'I ... I thought you were out,' was dragged from her—her voice uncertain for the first time as the words dropped away before she could gather herself together.

'Do you usually only take half an hour for lunch?'

'Occasionally.' She forced a note of detachment into her voice, glad her armour of calmness had come rushing to her aid.

'On the occasions you arrive late,' he said, making it a fact, not a question. 'You were on time this morning,' he stated when she didn't answer. 'Am I to anticipate that you will be half an hour late tomorrow morning?'

He was back to being sarcastic again. Gerry thought better than to remind him that she had told him first thing this morning that in future she would be in the office on the stroke of nine, since she wasn't at all certain she would be able to keep it up if he stayed in Layton for any length of time.

'I have a lot of typing to get through this afternoon,' she told him coldly.

'And you have no intention of working after five? He must be one hell of a fellow to have you dashing home every evening to get ready to meet him.'

Gerry looked away from him and concentrated on unfastening the keys she had locked together, wiping her fingers on a tissue afterwards in case any of the typing ink had adhered to them and smudged onto any of the papers.

'Where do you live, by the way?'

She wished he would go and leave her to get on with her work, but realised he could find out from staff records if he was that interested. 'Little Layton,' she told him, adding, though he probably knew anyway, 'It's a small village five miles outside of town.'

'You live with your parents?'

'My parents are dead.'

'I'm sorry.'

She had never expected to hear that gentle note in his voice. It surprised her into looking up. 'Thank you,' she said on a whisper, then her voice strengthening because something had to be done about this peculiar feeling that was starting up inside her at his unexpected sensitivity. 'I——' she began, but before she could continue, he was asking:

'When did they die?'

'My mother died when ... I was fifteen,' she nearly slipped up there and said 'we'. She and Teddy had always been 'we', but she didn't want anyone at Arrowsmiths asking questions about her home life, and certainly not Crawford Arrowsmith. She didn't want him knowing anything of what made her vulnerable. 'My father died last year.' She was unable to stop a bleak look from coming over her face as she thought of her father and the way he had died.

He had been out with Mark when the car had crashed,

killing Mark outright. Her father had lived for a few days—it had been thought he would make it, and Teddy, his favourite and six months pregnant, had gone to see him. Gerry had been there too and had seen Teddy crying to him that her beloved Mark was dead. But their father had relapsed the very next day and it had been Gerry who had been with him when he had died. He had known he was going to die. She had known it too and hadn't needed to hear the last words he had spoken—she would have done it anyway. 'Look after Teddy,' he'd breathed. 'She shouldn't be on her own.'

'It still hurts, doesn't it?' Gerry came crashing back to the present, and blinked twice so that Crawford Arrowsmith elucidated, 'It still hurts being without your father.'

Yes, it did hurt, particularly as there hadn't been time to mourn the dear man that he had been. All her energies had of necessity been concentrated in helping Teddy over that awful time.

'These things happen,' she said, striving to sound hard, but knowing she was making a very bad job of it. She wanted to end this conversation; she didn't want him digging into her private background—he couldn't be really interested anyway. Though she had to own he didn't sound as though he was being inquisitive purely for the sake of it. 'Have you had lunch?' she asked, hoping to divert him and at the same time imply that she would rather he went and had it than stand where he was looking down at her.

'Like you, I had a sandwich,' he said, which convinced her he must be able to see through wood panelling, because she had been by herself when she had eaten.

Just then the phone on her desk rang, cutting short any answer she would have made. He waited while she answered the phone, and she could have wished him back in his room with the door closed when she heard Teddy's voice coming across the wires. She felt stilted with him standing there looking ready to take in every word. And she wanted none of this to be in her voice while she spoke with Teddy. Teddy was quick to take offence these days and would be hurt if she thought it wasn't convenient to talk to her.

'Hello, love—how's your day going?' she asked, putting all the warmth she was able to into her voice under the circumstances. Crawford Arrowsmith would know from her words that it was a personal call, and she felt her anger rise that he made no move to go, but was openly listening to everything she said. Not that she had very much to say apart from making sympathetic noises at Teddy's tale of woe as she went on at length about Emma and Sarah's behaviour that morning.

At last Teddy came to the end of her account of her day so far, and wanted reassuring that Gerry wouldn't be late that night. 'I'll go round the bend if you're not here by half past five,' she wailed.

'Don't worry, Ted,' Gerry said soothingly. 'I'll be home by five-fifteen, I promise.' She felt rather than heard the sudden movement from Crawford Arrowsmith, but ignored him.

'You promise?' Teddy repeated.

'Yes, I promise, and you can put your feet up while I cook you something tasty—there'll be no need for you to do another thing for the rest of the evening.'

Gerry came off the phone feeling emotionally drained. Teddy didn't seem to be getting any better—she would have another talk to her tonight about going to see their doctor. Something would have to be done ...

'How old are you?'

She was jerked back to her surroundings by the coldest tones she had ever heard from a man. Crawford Arrowsmith's voice, apart from when he'd asked about her parents, had never been far from chilly, but now it was positively icy as he asked his question.

'Twenty-four,' she said without hesitation, and wanted

to ask why he wanted to know, but was stopped by the contemptuous look he was giving her.

'Twenty-four,' he repeated, still in the same icy tones. 'I would have thought a girl with your years would have had more sense than to make herself a doormat for any man.'

'What ...' she began, wondering if he had suddenly had a brainstorm.

'This Ted,' he said the name disparagingly, 'is obviously a layabout, otherwise he'd be at work—but instead of getting a meal ready for you when you arrive home, you have to get the meal ready, then pamper him by telling him he can put his feet up for the rest of the evening. Do you think your father would have approved?'

Never had she received such a lecture delivered in such icy tones. And even while it was sinking in that he thought she was living with some man called Ted, her anger at him daring to poke his nose into her personal life was rearing up and would not be suppressed.

'I'm sure my father would have approved whole-heartedly,' she said heatedly. 'But whether he would have done or not is no concern of yours. If I want to make a doormat of myself for Teddy I shall, and I'll thank you to keep your nose out of my affairs!'

His lip curled at her use of the word affair. 'Just you come in one minute after nine on any morning while I'm here, Miss Barton, and I'll make it my affair,' he told her threateningly, and stormed away from her to slam into his own office.

So now she knew—he had a 'thing' about people who made doormats of themselves—or was he old-fashioned enough not to like the idea of, as he thought in her case, a couple living together as man and wife without the benefit of a church service? She had no intention of putting him right on that score, and really the conclusion he had jumped to was rather amusing—though for the life of her she couldn't summon up a smile. She knew his anger had nothing to do with her personally—he wouldn't care a tinker's cuss whom she lived with. But his outburst had disquieted her all the same.

During the afternoon she was forced to go into his office over a query. She left it as long as she could knowing the less they saw of each other the better. Somehow he managed to get under her skin. Never once in the time she had been at Arrowsmiths had anyone seen beneath the surface of her—and he had only been here two days and twice she had let fly at him.

He was on the phone when she went in. Gerry gathered from what was being said it was a personal call and knowing her manners were better than his, made to go back to her own office until he had finished. But he waved her into the chair she had used earlier to take down his dictation, and went on with his call.

'I should think I could manage that,' he was saying, then as Gerry watched, his face transformed into humour as whoever was on the other end said something to amuse him. 'Now that was very naughty,' he said, and Gerry forgot any idea that there was anything old-fashioned about him at the intimacy of his tone. Not that she'd truly believed it in the first place, she thought, as she waited for him to finish his conversation. He looked too virile—too masculine. Much too much of everything that represented a hard-working, hard-playing, sophisticated man about town. Oh no, she'd like to bet he was far from celibate. 'In that case,' he was saying, 'I'll come up to town tonight. Wear something—er—casual.' He laughed again at something that was said in reply at the other end, said, 'I'll keep you to that,' and put down the phone.

His mood changed rapidly after that, as he became cool and overbearing as he dealt with her query. One good thing though, if he was going to London tonight—a two-hour drive by her calculations—he wouldn't want to hang around after five. Though how he could go on about her father disapproving of the way she was living, she had no idea. It was obvious to her from his telephone conversation that he wasn't making the two-hour drive in order to play Ludo when he got to whoever was at the other end.

He made short work of her query and handed the sheet of paper back to her. 'If you have any other queries, leave them until tomorrow—I don't want to be disturbed for the next hour,' he told her bluntly, without so much as looking at her. He didn't wait for her to answer, but reached for the papers in front of him, the gesture dismissal in itself.

Gerry needed all her control to get out of his office without hitting him. She didn't know why she should feel so violent towards him, but put it down to wounded pride that he could so summarily dismiss her as if she was of no account.

She checked the clock on the wall when she reached her desk. Four-fifteen. He said he didn't want to be disturbed for the next hour. Well, he wouldn't be. She had promised Teddy she would be home by five-fifteen and she fully intended to keep her promise.

At five minutes to five she was presented with a problem. The letters she had typed for him were of a very confidential nature. Whatever her personal feelings for him were, she couldn't possibly leave the letters lying waiting on her desk for him to sign, anybody could come in and see them. Her mind made up, she tidied her desk, then at one minute to five, with her handbag hanging over her arm, she collected the letters she had typed neatly together and without knocking entered his room.

He was deeply immersed in some figures before him and didn't look up. That suited her very well. Without again looking at him, she saw a cleared patch on his desk and placed the letters there to await his attention. Then as quietly as she had come in, she went out.

She was driving her car away from its parking space before she wondered how long it would be before he lifted his head and saw the correspondence she had left—she had a feeling he had been so deep in his work he didn't even know she had been in.

Both the babies were crying when she reached home. It was no uncommon happening for one to cry in sympathy with the other and Gerry entered the cottage wondering which one was the wounded soldier. Teddy too didn't seem very far from tears.

'Told you I'd make it for five-fifteen, didn't I?' Gerry said, forcing a note of calm into the pandemonium that reigned and taking one of the twins from Teddy so they had one each. She knew Teddy was struggling against tears and knew, heartless though it might seem to her, she couldn't show her the sympathy she was feeling or else there would be the four of them in tears.

'Another day like today and I'm sure I'll go bonkers,' Teddy said woefully. 'I'm not sure I'm not half way there already.'

'Now, Theodora,' Gerry used Teddy's given name, and tried a scoffing laugh at the same time, 'you're no more bonkers than I am,' she said bracingly while shushing the baby in her arms. 'You're just a wee bit run down, I expect.' Now seemed just the right moment to mention a visit to the doctor. 'We've got time—why don't we nip down and see Dr Bidley? He'll probably prescribe a tonic and you'll feel better in no time.'

It gave her some indication of how Teddy was feeling to hear her say, 'Do you think that's all I need?'

'I'm positive.' Gerry held her breath. Teddy had always shunned having a doctor take a look at her—this was a delicate moment. She couldn't force her sister to see a doctor, but in her view it was important she see Dr Bidley. 'It wouldn't take us five minutes in the car and we could ask

him to check on Sarah's teething—I didn't tell you, but she
was quite fretful during the night.'

'Oh, Gerry, I'm a selfish pig—I never heard a sound,
and we share the same room ...' Teddy looked as though
she was going to burst into tears.

'Shall we go, then?' Gerry put in quickly—having got
Teddy this far towards agreeing to see Dr Bidley, she
didn't want to lose any ground.

'We'll go and see him about Sarah, he can have a look
at Emma as well,' was as far as Teddy would compromise.

There were several people in the village surgery and
they exchanged good evenings as they went in. The twins
had ceased their crying and looked around the cream-
emulsioned walls with interest, completely breaking the ice
in the waiting room with their charming gurgles, and soon
there was a steady hum of chatter as they waited their
turn to go in.

When they went in, Gerry carrying Emma and Teddy
carrying Sarah, they found it was not Dr Bidley, who had
seen Teddy through her difficult confinement, but a much
younger man who looked to be not more than thirty. His
twinkling blue eyes in no way endeared him to Teddy,
though. She told him who they were, then asked sharply:

'Where's Dr Bidley?'

Gerry heard the aggressive note in her voice and hoped
the new doctor wasn't easily offended. Teddy wasn't often
aggressive these days, but it looked as though she'd taken
an immediate dislike to the new man.

'Dr Bidley is taking a well-earned holiday,' he replied,
seeming in no way put out as he addressed Teddy, his
professional eyes taking in more than she knew. 'He's gone
to visit his son in Australia, so I'm afraid you'll have to put
up with me for three months.' They made quite a crowd
in the small consulting room. 'I'm Paul Meadows, by the
way—now which one of you is here to see me—I have
quite a busy evening.'

'It's Sarah—she's teething,' Teddy told him, thrusting the baby at him, and in case he had any idea of asking Gerry and Emma to leave and so give him more space in the room, she said, 'I'm a widow—my sister comes everywhere with me.'

'Does she indeed—and does your sister ever go anywhere by herself?' He had taken Sarah from her and was checking her over.

'She doesn't need to—we're quite happy the way we are.'

Dr Meadows didn't answer her, but continued to examine Sarah. 'How old are the twins?' he asked after a moment.

Gerry kept quiet, letting Teddy do all the talking. She felt her confidence growing in this man who gave Sarah back to Teddy and promptly lifted Emma out of her arms and proceeded to examine her the way he had done Sarah. She had a feeling he saw far more than any words she could have found to explain that Teddy needed his help.

She received the shock of her life, though, when he handed Emma back to her to find it was her he turned his attention to and not Teddy as she had been waiting for.

'And what about you?' he asked, and she turned her startled eyes to him.

'I'm perfectly well,' she began. 'It's T ...'

'How much do you weigh?'

'I haven't weighed myself in ages,' Gerry told him. 'But it's not me ...'

'How's your appetite?'

By now Teddy was turning and taking notice, seeming to see for the first time that Gerry had lost weight, while her own weight after the children had been born had returned to normal.

Then Paul Meadows was pulling down Gerry's lower eyelids and saying a course of iron tablets wouldn't go amiss.

'What's wrong with her?' That was Teddy, for the first time in an age coming the older sister—which she was by twenty minutes.

'Without examining her completely I'd say she was on the way to becoming thoroughly worn out,' he said, not making any bones about it.

Gerry started to say, 'I'm all right,' but Teddy seemed to be so completely shaken, she was answering the doctor's questions like a lamb, and they seemed to have forgotten completely that the subject of their discussion was standing there with them. Even the twins seemed to be listening intently—they were quiet for the moment at any rate.

'And Miss Barton is the breadwinner for all of you?' he was asking.

Gerry's astonishment at this turn of events was disappearing; she wanted to tell him not to ask Teddy these questions. Teddy wasn't well—she needed protecting. Before, her father had always spoiled her, seen to it that no harm came to Teddy, then Mark had cosseted and loved her. Teddy needed to be looked after—yet here was this new doctor completely unaware of Teddy's needs telling Teddy she would have to look after Miss Barton if she didn't want her to be ill.

Teddy looked as stunned as Gerry felt, but Gerry was the first to recover as the doctor bade them good evening. In a flash she had handed Emma over to her sister, opened the door for her, and with an, 'I'll join you in a moment, Teddy,' she closed the door behind her and turned back to Dr Meadows.

'The twins are very healthy specimens,' Paul Meadows said as if he thought that was what she wanted to talk to him about.

'I know that,' Gerry said. She was the one who brought them down regularly for Dr Bidley to check on. 'It's Teddy who isn't well.'

'There's nothing wrong with that young woman that a

healthy outside interest wouldn't cure.'

'But she's been so tired lately—so tearful. Teddy's had an awful time getting over the loss of her husband.'

'She's bored,' Paul Meadows came back, and Gerry had a feeling she wasn't getting through to him.

'Bored?' she echoed, feeling a tingle of guilt that their finances didn't stretch to very exciting outings.

'At a guess I'd say before her husband died she was never still for more than five minutes at a time.' He looked enquiringly at her, his blue eyes solemn for the moment.

'Well, yes, I suppose you're right,' Gerry admitted. Even Teddy's pregnancy hadn't stopped her from going to parties—all that had ceased when Mark had died.

'It seems to me, Miss Barton, that since Mrs Wilson's husband died, you've had a fair try at exhausting yourself in a mistaken attempt to make up to her all she has lost. While I can understand the close bond between you, it just won't do, you know. I can appreciate that there must be times when the twins drive her up the wall, but that's fairly normal—most babies are trying from time to time. But if you're to continue to support the family, I strongly advise you to start taking care of yourself. Take it from me, you're the one who needs looking after, not Mrs Wilson.'

The twins were howling when Gerry joined Teddy outside, and it wasn't until Emma and Sarah were in bed and peace reigned once more that Gerry was able to talk to her sister about the visit to the doctor. She felt dreadfully guilty about the whole thing since her only reason for going had been in order that Teddy should have professional advice.

'Of course Dr Meadows has got it all wrong,' she said as she peeled some potatoes. Teddy had joined her in the kitchen and was helping with the meal—that in itself was rare because at this time in the evening with the children in bed, Teddy usually flopped down on the settee declaring herself 'frazzled'. Teddy pottering around the kitchen when she should be resting in no way lessened Gerry's feeling of guilt.

'I don't know,' Teddy said thoughtfully. 'I hadn't noticed before—but you are a bit scraggy.'

Gerry's guilt dissolved into laugher. 'With that kind of sisterly remark, I reckon I can do without your help in the kitchen!'

Teddy's own laughter joined hers, and Gerry was arrested by it. Teddy hadn't laughed very much lately— and she gave sufficient thought to wonder if Paul Meadows' tonic hadn't needed to come out of a medicine bottle.

CHAPTER THREE

HAVING set her alarm to go off fifteen minutes earlier than usual, Gerry was in a deep sleep when the clamour of the alarm roused her the next morning. In view of Crawford Arrowsmith saying he would make it his affair if she arrived late at the office she couldn't afford to risk arriving so much as one minute after nine. She hoped he'd be in a better mood this morning than he had been in yesterday. He hadn't been any too sweet before Teddy's phone call—afterwards he had been positively impossible. Still, perhaps his visit 'up to town' last night had sweetened him; she had to smile as she poured some tea and wondered if there was sufficient sugar in the world to do that job!

Sarah, whom she had set down for a minute while she took a hurried sip of tea, crawled off on an investigatory recce, and with one eye on the clock Gerry went to fetch her back, only to be forestalled as Sarah's head came into contact with something solid. She hadn't really hurt herself but sent up a shriek of protest just the same and began to cry as Gerry went to pick her up.

'Oh, my darling,' she cooed, giving the damp bundle a hug, 'what a nasty chair to hurt you!' She carried her back into the kitchen to take another hasty glance at the clock. Sarah had been whimpering for attention when she'd left the bathroom earlier, and Gerry had changed her only ten minutes ago, and already she was damp again. Did she have time to put a fresh nappy on the child? She couldn't very well leave her like that. Wondering if she could slip in without the eagle eye of Crawford Arrowsmith spotting her and knowing she was on a loser, she was just about to go in search of a fresh nappy when Teddy emerged in her dressing gown, asking what the time was.

'Bang goes the first of my good intentions,' Teddy told her, holding out her arms to receive Sarah, who had forgotten all about her tears on seeing her mother. 'I fully intended being first up this morning,' Teddy went on, seeming to be more cheerful than she had in months. 'You're damp,' she said abstractedly to Sarah, planting a kiss on top of her head before turning her attention back to Gerry. 'And you're going to be late if you don't look sharp.'

Gerry's mouth almost dropped open at that. Never before had Teddy shown the slightest concern whether she was late or not. 'You're right,' she said, recovering fast. 'Anything you want bringing home?'

'I'll give you a ring if I think of anything.'

Gerry set the car in motion trying not to be too overjoyed at the difference in Teddy this morning. On other occasions she had left Teddy in a fairly cheerful frame of mind, only to find her in floods of tears when she arrived home.

Patting herself on the back that for three mornings in a row she had made it to the office for nine, Gerry reached the door to her office, donned her cloak of cool unflap-

pability, and went in. Her first glance showed her Crawford Arrowsmith had not come in yet, and when at nine-
fifteen he still hadn't appeared, she realised she needn't
have been so anxious to get there for nine after all. He had
probably enjoyed himself so much in London he had
overslept, she thought sourly, then forgot about him and
got on with some work.

It was odd, though, the way her thoughts would go
back to him again and again during the day. Probably because she was nowhere near as rushed today as she had
been yesterday—and anyway, she consoled herself, since
she had to go into the office he had used every time she
wanted to check on something that was housed in that
room, it was only natural that he should come to mind.
When she found herself wondering what his companion
of last evening looked like, though, she hurriedly blanked
her mind off; she wasn't remotely interested.

Basil Dyer came to see her during the afternoon. 'I know
the coast is clear,' he said, which effectively told her he
wouldn't have come in for a chat if Crawford had been
there. 'Just had a phone call from our beloved leader about
some figures—he rang from head office.'

So he was working in London today. It wouldn't have
crossed his mind, of course, to put through a call to her
to say he wouldn't be in. Not that she wanted to hear his
voice—perish the thought! She wondered if he was still
angry with her for being a 'doormat', then forgot about
him as Basil went on to ask how she was getting on.

'Still a little at sixes and sevens, I expect,' Basil sum-
mised. 'Mr Arrowsmith's cousin, William Hudson, is being tipped for the Company Secretary's job. Nothing like
keeping it in the family.'

'He doesn't work here, does he?' She'd never heard the
name before and was amazed how Basil managed to ferret
out his information—in general it was usually pretty
accurate.

'No—been learning the business up at head office, I think. Still, we'll have to wait and see.'

Gerry went home that night, glad Basil Dyer had been in to see her. His visit had successfully broken up her day since Teddy hadn't telephoned.

Teddy seemed as bright that night as she had been in the morning, and Gerry went to bed that night with hope in her heart that her sister might at last be showing some signs of returning to the girl she used to be. Though she knew it was too early yet to dare to uncross her fingers.

She went to work the next morning glad that it was Friday. She had no way of knowing if Crawford Arrowsmith would be in, but if he was, and was the same unbearable brute he had been the last time she had seen him, then she had the whole of Saturday and Sunday in which to get over it. She was on time again today—only just, though, having been up half the night with Sarah and sleeping through her alarm. She shuddered to think how late she would have been if Emma hadn't sent up a wail for attention, for Teddy hadn't heard a sound.

Crawford Arrowsmith had returned, she saw as she went into her office. He was seated behind his desk the way he had been when she had left the night before last, and was as deeply immersed now as he had been then in whatever he was working on. Well, if he wasn't going to raise his head to wish her good morning, she wasn't going to intrude.

She felt a tenseness come over her as she sat before her typewriter. If he didn't give her something to do soon, she would soon be out of work, and the last thing she wanted to do was ask him for something.

'Will you come through, Miss Barton.'

His voice reached her when she was on the last of her jobs. She saw it would be idiotic to use the intercom when the door to the two offices stood open. She had thought he might get up and close it when she'd started typing, but he hadn't. Full marks to you for concentration, she thought, as she picked up her notepad and pencil.

He gave her a hard look when she was seated before him. 'What have you been doing with yourself—you look washed out?' He was all aggression.

Thanks very much! she thought. What with Teddy saying she looked scraggy, and him telling her she looked washed out, it did her ego a power of good. He then seemed to regret having made a personal remark, for without further ado, not waiting for any reply she might have made, he proceeded to give her rapid dictation in an unbroken flow that made her feel if he didn't stop soon, she would have to interrupt him while she got the cramp out of her fingers. She was saved the necessity of doing that when he came to the end of what he was saying. And since it looked as though that was all he had for her, she made to rise.

'Don't go for a moment—I haven't finished with you yet.'

That sounded ominous. Gerry subsided back on to her chair. At least her fingers were having a rest while she waited for what else she was to take down. But it wasn't dictation he had to give her, but information about her future.

'From what I've seen of your work so far, you appear to be a fairly competent P.A.,' he began. She knew without false modesty that she was good, but it didn't appear he was ready to go that far—though, she supposed in fairness, the P.A.s he employed in London were pretty streamlined. 'I told you at the beginning of the week that you would be redundant from this particular job,' he went on. Gerry waited, trying not to let her anxiety show. It seemed she would learn any moment now to which department she would be assigned. 'After seeing some of your work I'm inclined to believe I may have been somewhat hasty in my decision,' he ended, to her astonishment.

Gerry felt her heartbeats quicken that this icy man in front of her could be big enough to indicate he might have made a mistake. Keeping her face as expressionless as possible wasn't easy as the thought roared through her that perhaps he might agree to her staying on in her old job. She did hope so. She was sure to get the same money she was getting now—if they moved her to a department that didn't pay so well heaven alone knew how she and Teddy would manage. Besides which, she had seen a new side to the work since he had taken over, and it now seemed more interesting than the work Mr Gillett had given her to do. Aware that her air of calm was in danger of slipping, she sat upright on her chair, her legs neatly crossed at the ankles as she gave him her attention. There was a pause between them which lengthened, and she was conscious he was giving her face a cold, unsmiling scrutiny. It unnerved her, and where she should have remained quiet and allowed him to finish, she found herself asking:

'Are you saying I can keep my job? That I can still be P.A. to the Company Secretary?'

His expression didn't alter, though he leaned back in his chair, showing he was very much at ease, very much in charge, while she was becoming more and more tense with every second as she waited for his answer.

'With certain provisos,' he tossed at her.

Here we go, she thought, getting herself ready for a lecture on her timekeeping. 'I've been early every day this week,' she blurted out, then could have bitten her tongue at his sarcastic answer.

'I'll see you get a medal.' Then getting down to brass tacks, 'All being well the new man will take over some time next month. His name is William Hudson,' so Basil had been right yet again. 'I think you should work well together. But,' he paused, and she tensed at that, because there seemed to be an ominous threat in that small word. 'But I'm rather afraid you may have picked up ways from

William's predecessor that are not in accordance with the way I want things done.'

Gerry wanted to protest that everyone had their own way of working, but could see the futility of that argument. True enough, she had worked in the way Mr Gillett had wanted, and probably had, she was prepared to concede, picked up bad habits. On Mr Gillett's instruction she had taken short cuts which were not her style at all, but since she badly needed this job, she was fully prepared to take heed of what Crawford Arrowsmith was telling her. If he wanted the work doing without the aid of short-cutting, she was prepared to go along with him all the way.

'I'm adaptable,' she said quietly. 'If you want the routine altered I'm in agreement with anything you suggest.'

He looked at her levelly, and she had a suspicion there was a gleam in his eye, like someone about to play a trump card, but nothing prepared her for his next statement.

'Good,' he said briefly. 'I'm sure you're a young woman who means what she says. That being the case you will, I know, have no objection to spending two or three days at our London office seeing the way things work there.'

'London!' she gasped, all calm gone from her now as her brain took in what was involved with Teddy for her to spend a couple of nights away from home. Annoyingly that unruly strand of hair had started to slip again and lay in a wave against the side of her face, as she tried desperately to remove her flabbergasted expression.

'Yes—London,' Crawford Arrowsmith said, noting her astonishment and adding sarcastically, 'Did you think I said Mars?'

'But I can't!' she said, ignoring his sarcasm. Apart from the fact that Teddy couldn't bear to be on her own at night—even in her teens she had needed other people around her at night—Teddy would never cope on her own.

'If you want this job you can.' The sarcasm had gone from him now, leaving him cold and ruthless. 'What's the matter—is there a queue waiting to have feet wiped all over them? Are you afraid your lover will find he can do without you if you go away for a few nights?'

Gerry stood up. She didn't have to take this. He was thoroughly enjoying seeing her squirm—he knew he had her in a cleft stick.

'Sit down.' He said it quite mildly, but there was an authority in his voice that had her sitting when what she would have liked to do was hit that cold disdainful expression from off his face. 'Accommodation has been booked for you,' he told her, mentioning the name of the hotel, and seeming not to notice the sparks of anger flashing in her eyes at his previous remark. 'You will travel on Sunday in order to report to our London offices at nine on Monday morning. You will stay in London on Monday night and Tuesday night, and if by Wednesday you've got the hang of how things are run that end, you may then return to Layton——— Is that clear?'

Gerry knew she dared not argue with anything he had said if she wanted to keep this P.A. job that paid so well, though she looked forward to some far distant date when she could tell him exactly what she thought of his overbearing, arrogant, ruthless tactics. There was mutiny in every line of her body as she realised she had no choice but to agree to do what he wanted.

'Yes—everything's clear,' she said through tight lips, and stood up. Somehow she had to find a way of getting out of this, but at the moment she couldn't think of a thing.

Crawford's voice stopped her as she would have stormed out of his office. 'You're dying to tell me to go to hell, aren't you?' he questioned, and could see from the flame in her eyes how accurate his question had been. 'You must love this—Ted person very much,' he added, and there was a note in his voice she didn't understand—which was just as well, she thought, since he understood enough about her to know if it wasn't for Teddy, she'd have told him exactly where to go.

'I do,' she said quietly, and left the room closing the door behind her.

Perhaps it was a good thing the whole of her concentration was needed on transcribing the shorthand she had taken earlier. For it gave her little time to ponder on how she was going to spend three nights in London—more if, as he had intimated, she hadn't got the hang of the way things were run. She didn't see how she could possibly leave Teddy to cope on her own, and since they kept themselves to themselves, there wasn't anyone in the village she knew well enough to ask to stay with her sister and the twins overnight.

It was nearly lunch time when Teddy rang asking her to get some cotton wool in her lunch hour, and Gerry was glad that the door between the two offices was closed and Crawford Arrowsmith wasn't in earshot to give her some more of his sarcasm for being a doormat when she finished the call.

'Everything all right?' Teddy seemed to be coping quite well since their visit to Paul Meadows. Teddy assured her everything was fine.

'The twins, for once in their lives, have both decided to go to sleep at the same time,' Teddy told her with a little exaggeration. 'So I'm taking advantage of that and am going to have five minutes myself.'

It was wonderful to hear Teddy without that tearful note in her voice as she said goodbye. It had been pure cowardice on her part, Gerry thought, as she put down the phone, that she hadn't been able to tell her she was being sent to London for a few days.

Feeling the results of her broken night catching up on her, she took almost the whole of her lunch hour to relax and unwind. It would mean she'd have to go full pelt this afternoon, but she felt a weariness come over her and even though she was loath to give in to it, thought she might be more use to Teddy tonight if she relaxed now.

She had seen little of Crawford Arrowsmith since he had delivered his bombshell earlier, apart from knowing he had passed her desk unspeaking a couple of times during the afternoon. And when she took his letters in for signature at half past four, she would have left them on his desk as she had done before, but he told her to wait while he signed them, then she could take them up to the post room.

'Did I say that?' He pushed a letter along the desk to where she was standing.

Gerry took the letter up and read what had so obviously offended him. 'In connection with yours of the fourteenth ultimo,' she read, feeling a tide of pink colour come up under her skin that he should have to pull her up. It didn't help to know he had turned in his chair and was watching her.

'I'm sorry,' she said, knowing he had dictated no such thing. Her concentration hadn't been as great as she had thought, with the nagging worry of leaving Teddy intruding every so often. Mr Gillett had often started his letters in that stiff, creaking way, and she must have typed it automatically. 'I'll type it again,' she said, and regretted now taking nearly all of her lunch hour, when only half an hour would have put her so much further ahead.

'It's no great crime,' he said unexpectedly, causing her to turn to catch his slate grey eyes watching her embarrassed colour subside. 'Though I'll agree it will have to be typed again.'

She stood and waited while he checked the rest of the correspondence she had typed, and wanted to disappear through the floorboards when he found another two glaring errors. But to her amazement his tone was quite mild when he pointed these out to her and said he would like them retyped too.

What a strange man he was, she thought, as she returned to her typewriter. She would have expected any other reaction from him at her blatant incompetence—she didn't think her obvious embarrassment had anything to do with the lack of anger in his voice when he had spoken to her—but she had seen another side of him she would never have suspected existed.

Having retyped the offending letters, she read them through carefully. Satisfied he could have no quarrel with the result, she prepared to take the letters in to him. First, though, she checked the clock and saw to her horror it was ten past five. Where the time had gone she had no idea, but it was a certainty she wouldn't be home at the expected five-fifteen. Her fingers were automatically dialling Honeysuckle Cottage before she was aware she had lifted the phone. Gerry's spirits sank that just as Teddy's voice voice answered the communicating door opened and Crawford Arrowsmith came in.

'Hello,' said Teddy, having given her number and hearing nothing in response.

'Oh—hello, Ted,' Gerry came back, tearing her eyes away from those slate grey ones that seemed to visibly harden as he heard whom she was telephoning. 'Sorry to be so late in ringing you, but I'll be about fifteen minutes late.' There was a silence at the other end and Gerry was torn between a desire to soothe her sister and a desire to hurriedly finish the call, for Crawford Arrowsmith was looking at her as if he would like to snatch the phone out of her hand and slam it back on its rest. She tore her eyes away from him, hating that he had the power to make her feel so agitated. 'All right, love?'

Teddy hadn't been all that pleased, Gerry could tell that from her tone, but she hadn't begun to weep as a week ago she might have done. Then there was no further time to worry about Teddy, for Crawford Arrowsmith had stretched out a hand and picked up the letters she had been going to take in to him.

'Since you'll be a threadbare doormat if you don't get home to dear Ted soon, you'd better go now,' he said shortly.

Her eyes flew to his, but there was no answering spark of anger in his cold eyes, just an expression of disgust, that unaccountably defused her anger and made her heart lurch that he could think her so lacking in moral fibre.

She watched the back of him disappear into his own office, saw the door close quietly, and didn't move for some seconds. He thinks I'm weak, she thought, and for no reason, when she had been at pains to keep her home life and business life separate, she would have dearly loved to follow him and explain that Teddy was her sister.

Of course, she soon got over that feeling once she was in her car and on her way to Little Layton. He would have thought her a complete idiot anyway, she mused, as she negotiated a tight bend. He wasn't remotely interested in her home life—would in turn probably be highly embarrassed at her confiding in him. Though she couldn't quite see him being embarrassed about anything. She forgot about him as she turned the car on to the earth drive beside the cottage, though she couldn't help wondering briefly that he had said no more about London. Obviously, she decided, once he had made his wishes known he had thought no more about it—it would never occur to him that his orders might be disobeyed. Now what was she going to tell Teddy—and more important still, how was Teddy going to take it?

Teddy didn't take it very well at all. The evening had been spent much the same as usual in getting the twins to bed, clearing away their toys, having their own meal, tidying up and washing. Up until the point when they both sat down at last, Teddy had made an effort and worked alongside Gerry and the evening had been without stress. Gerry felt a glow inside that Teddy seemed to be making

progress and felt easier than she had been at bringing up
the subject.

'London?' Teddy ejaculated when she told her, react-
ing in much the same way she herself had done when
Crawford Arrowsmith had delivered his ultimatum. 'You
mean *stay* there?' Teddy sounded so incredulous, Gerry
cut in quickly, trying to calm the situation before Teddy
had hysterics.

'It'll only be for three days,' she said, trying to soothe
her down.

But Teddy wasn't to be soothed, and amidst floods of
tears sobbed out that she couldn't be left on her own overnight. 'I know I'm selfish,' she cried, 'and I've tried really
hard since that Paul Meadows shocked me into seeing
you're the one who needs looking after, b-but honestly,
Gerry, I'll go mad if I have to stay here for three whole
days and nights by myself!'

No matter what Gerry said or did, there was no calm-
ing her sister, and knowing she would soon be crying with
her if Teddy didn't stop soon, she went into the kitchen
and made a cup of tea neither of them would want, and
puzzled her brain while waiting for it to brew on what to
do. But her mind was so tired, so confused, her emotions
so churned up as they had been through the day ever
since Crawford Arrowsmith had told her if she wanted the
job she would do as he said, that nothing came through
that would answer the problem.

That was until she returned to the living room with the
tray of tea. She looked across at Teddy, so forlorn and unhappy, and unable to bear the sight of her sister looking
so miserable, she glanced to the window and saw her beat
up old A35 standing on the drive.

'I could travel each day, I suppose,' she said, not looking forward to the normally two-hour drive that would
probably take three hours in her car, but warming to the

idea as Teddy stopped crying for a moment and looked at her with hope in her eyes.

'Could you, Gerry?' she asked quietly. 'I wouldn't mind how late you got back provided you came home at night—I'd do all the work and have a meal ready for when you come in.' Teddy was prepared to promise anything rather than be left on her own at night.

Gerry wasn't sure the A35 would last the pace. It was on its last legs now, having only just scraped through its M.O.T. ten months ago. Her mind refused to wrestle with the problem of what to do for transport if the car didn't pass its next M.O.T. test; she secretly knew it wouldn't. Aside from the little trips out Teddy looked forward to at weekends, the infrequent bus service would make it impossible for her to get to and from work.

'Do it, Gerry,' Teddy was urging. 'I'll get up early with you in the mornings,' she promised, 'and it will only be for a couple of days—you said so yourself—and it's light at nights now until after ten, so you won't be driving home in the dark.'

It was settled. Gerry had known that once she had told Teddy her idea there would be no backing down.

On Sunday she pressed her best suit. It had been a good one once. She hadn't worn it for some time—but she wanted to look smart tomorrow when she met some of the staff at the London office. Teddy insisted she go to bed early that night, since in order to arrive at the parent company of Arrowsmith Computers in London for nine, she would have to leave Little Layton no later than six the next morning.

The suit she had pressed last night didn't look anywhere near as smart as she had remembered it when she put it on the following morning. At one time it had fitted her snugly, but as she looked at her reflection in the mirror, Gerry saw that it now positively hung on her. She'd so wanted to look smart today too, she sighed. It couldn't be helped, and anyway there were more pressing problems than the way she looked.

True to her word, Teddy was up to see her off, but only because she had made Gerry promise to wake her. And when Gerry said she couldn't possibly eat breakfast at that unearthly hour, Teddy herself packed her a small parcel of sandwiches.

'I'll get back as soon as I can,' Gerry promised as her sister came out in her dressing gown to the car with her. 'Why don't you go back to bed—you might get another hour or two before the twins wake up?'

With Teddy's, 'I think I will,' ringing in her ears, Gerry let in the clutch and pulled off the drive.

She convinced herself as she tootled through hamlet after hamlet—not daring to take the A35 on the motorway and let herself in for untold expense if the car broke down —that she really enjoyed what she was doing. Crawford Arrowsmith would never know, and it was quite a treat to have the roads almost to herself. There were one or two steep hills en route she hadn't anticipated, and she praised the A35 out loud—'Good girl!' she said as the old car responded to her coaxing, and made it every time. But she needed all her concentration when she neared London. The weekend had been spent in poring over old maps of Mark's they had found, but even so the traffic here was thicker. She began to feel edgy when her watch showed her time was going on. Then, as she had planned last night, she found a place to park on the outskirts of London, and minutes later was boarding a tube that seemed to take a very short time to take her almost to her destination.

Gerry felt quite pleased with herself when she stepped through the wide impressive entrance of Arrowsmith Computers with fifteen minutes to spare. If the early start, the concentration required on her driving, and the rush and bustle of London—so much a change from the sleepy backwater of Little Layton—had caused her temples to pound, she was going to be the only one to know it, she decided as she went up to the enquiry desk where a smart young lady was already on duty, and made her enquiry.

'Ah yes—you'll want Miss Langley.' The girl smiled at her as if pleased to welcome a member from their Layton company. 'I don't suppose she'll be in yet. If you'd like to take the lift to the rest room, I'll tell her you're here when she arrives.'

Gerry found the rest room without too much difficulty. It was very little different from the rest room in Layton, except that it was larger and had a few more tables and easy chairs. She selected one of the chairs near to the door, and sank down into it gratefully, glad to be able to close her eyes for a few minutes.

'Do I take it your hotel bed wasn't so comfortable that you have to finish off your sleep here?'

Gerry woke up with a start. Crawford Arrowsmith's voice had been the last one she had expected to hear, but it brought her round from her ten-minute nap quicker than anything else could have done. It was like having a douche of cold water thrown over her, she thought in a bemused way, as she hurriedly shook the remnants of sleep away. As she made to get up from the cosiness of her chair her hands went to her hair to check that it was still neatly in its bun. She felt at a decided disadvantage anyway without having to stretch her neck to look up at him.

'Do you always dress your hair that way?' Crawford was asking as she stood up, his personal remark causing her to glance at him. He was standing close to her and it unnerved her, so she took a step away from him while she gathered her scattered wits about her.

'Are you suggesting I wear my hair flowing over my shoulders while I'm at business?' She was rather proud of her cool tones.

'It would be an improvement,' he said shortly, opening the door indicating that she should follow him. 'But then

anything would be an improvement to the hideous style
you favour at the moment.'

Because of his long strides she was forced to walk
quickly to keep up with him as he turned a corner and
strode out along another corridor, then through a pair of
swing doors. She thought he had finished with the subject
of her hair and began to wonder how she was going to
cope with what this Miss Langley was going to show her
today—it couldn't be very much different from what she
had been doing in Layton . . .

'I think you try to make yourself unattractive on pur-
pose,' he said, coming to a halt so suddenly she almost
bumped into him.

'I . . .' Again she stepped a pace away from him, and
found herself staring up into cold grey eyes, whatever she
had been going to say lost as the irritation she realised he
was feeling with her showed in his face.

'I think this fellow you're living with is so unsure of
you he makes you wear clothes that are too big for you—
clothes that hide the curves beneath,' Crawford Arrowsmith said so outrageously that Gerry almost exploded,
would have done she knew, but for an unexpected gleam
in his eyes that gave her the oddest idea that he was deliberately goading her, deliberately trying to get her to lose
her temper. It was as if he was trying to find out what was
on the other side of her, she thought, and couldn't think
why he should bother, other than that he was so arrogant
he had to know what made everybody tick.

Not without difficulty, she swallowed her wrath. She'd
known before today that he had an uncanny knack of making her forget her determination to be outwardly cool.

'You can think what the hell you like, Mr Arrowsmith,'
she said sweetly. 'If I choose to dress in ex-Army surplus
it has nothing to do with you.'

She expected him to jump down her throat as her words
reached him, but to her surprise, she espied a gleam of

admiration in his eyes, and knew he wasn't deceived by her sweetness.

'Tell your lover the next time you see him that nothing can hide the beauty of your bone structure,' he said to her growing amazement, adding coolly. 'Your hair may resemble some schoolmarm from the nineteen-twenties, but scraped back from your face the way it is, it shows up your beauty to anyone with an eye for that sort of thing.' He then continued to walk on, and Gerry was forced to walk on with him, while her mind tried to sort out whether he had an eye for 'that sort of thing', or if he was once more trying to get a rise out of her.

Then there was no time to draw any conclusion from what he had said, for he stopped as they came up to a door painted in the palest of greys, and walked in, and when she had followed he closed the door with a very definite click.

At the very least Gerry expected to see the unknown Miss Langley there. But on staring round the room, she saw there was no one there but their two selves. She looked about her as if expecting to find Miss Langley hiding in one of the corners while a definite conviction passed through her that she wouldn't find Miss Langley here, because this office belonged not to her opposite number in London, but to the head of Arrowsmiths himself ... the man who was now leaning idly against the solid wood of the only desk in the thickly carpeted room with its pale green walls. The man who was now looking at her from across the space of a few yards, with a look in his eyes that said he had some very strong words to say to her—and if she wasn't mistaken, she was going to be made to listen to every one of them.

'I ... er ... thought you were taking me to see Miss Langley,' she said after a long moment, hating the fact he had seen her swallow before she had found her voice.

'All in good time, Miss Barton—all in good time. First

of all, though, I think you and I need to have a little chat.'
She didn't like at all the steel she heard lurking behind
the mildness of his words. 'Perhaps you would like to take
a seat.'

CHAPTER FOUR

GERRY elected to take one of the two hard-backed chairs in
the room, feeling suddenly the need to sit down as Crawford Arrowsmith continued to give her his cool appraisal.
He made no move to take the seat behind the desk and
she wished he would, for with him on her side of the desk
—barely a yard away—he was much too close for comfort.

She tried composing her face into remote lines, adopt-
ing a 'nothing you can say can upset me' manner. But
when the silence in the room lengthened and he still hadn't
said a word, she was forced by the very disturbance somewhere in her middle to look at him, and hated that without so much as saying a word, he had the power to
unnerve her. His slate grey eyes were boring into her and
she knew she wouldn't be able to take it much longer—
any minute now she would be losing the temper that was
rarely in evidence.

'You—you said you wanted to speak to me?' It that
wasn't pointed enough, she thought, hating that he was
propped up against the desk and in a position to look down
his straight nose at her, then he must be being deliberately
obtuse.

'How long is it since you had a check-up?'

What she had expected him to say she wasn't sure, but
that was the last thing that would have come to her mind.
'You mean . . .'

'I mean when was the last time you saw a doctor?'

Oh heavens, she hoped he wasn't going to go on about what he called her washed-out appearance. Arrowsmiths had their own medical unit—she had a nasty feeling if she didn't give him the right answer to his question he would be bundling her along to see the firm's doctor before she got as far as seeing Miss Langley.

'As a matter of fact I was in the doctor's surgery last week.' She couldn't help but feel smug as she trotted out that piece of information, safe in the knowledge that she had well and truly spiked his guns.

'I see.' He looked at her consideringly, to her annoyance seeming in no way at all put out. 'And what was your doctor's verdict?'

Still feeling she had scored one over him, she decided she could afford to be flippant. 'He said I was as well as could be expected.' She wished afterwards she had held her tongue. For with a speed she hadn't anticipated he left the desk he had been so negligently leaning against and was standing over her, his hands gripping her shoulders with such painful intensity she thought her bones would break.

'You're pregnant,' he accused, his eyes glaring down at her as though she had done him a personal injury.

'I'm not!' She tried to inject a light laugh into her voice, anything to ease the tenseness of the situation. But the laugh didn't come off, as the fear his blazing look sent through her, cancelled every other emotion. 'I'm not,' she said again, when his hands continued to grip her in their punishing hold. 'Y-you're hurting me,' she stammered, while wondering what on earth had got into him. It couldn't matter a hoot to him whether she was pregnant or not other than that he'd have to find another P.A. to work for his cousin when he came to Layton.

Crawford Arrowsmith let go the brutal hold he had on her, and she would dearly love to rub her bruised shoulders, but something—she didn't know what—stopped her. Perhaps it was because he was looking at her as though only then realising the pain he had inflicted on her —and for no reason she could think of she didn't want to make more of it than he knew it to be.

'I'm ... forgive me, I——' He didn't finish what he was saying, but returned to being the overpowering, arrogant man she knew him to be as this time he went to the other side of the desk and took the seat facing her, as if only by having the desk between them would he be able to keep his hands off her. This disturbed Gerry more than if he'd gone to lean against the desk in front of her again. Although she couldn't say with any truth that she was very close to anyone—other than Teddy and the twins of course —she hadn't thought she aroused such feelings of dislike in anyone that they had to make a special effort to keep themselves from committing a physical violence on her. And it was so obvious that Crawford Arrowsmith didn't like her that she felt almost like fainting as the impact of the effect she had on him hit her.

Before she had time to think further why it should bother her that he couldn't stand the sight of her, she saw his blazing look had vanished, and he was now giving her the benefit of the coldest scrutiny she had ever encountered—which did nothing to detract from the very clear impression he had given her that he would rather have her room than her company.

'So you're telling me there's no need to send you along to our medical centre,' he stated coldly, confirming her thought that he had that idea in mind.

'No need at all,' she confirmed quietly.

'Good.' It seemed he was all set to dismiss the subject, he changed the conversation so quickly, Gerry had to race her mind to catch up with him. 'You found your hotel without any difficulty?'

'I ...' She stopped. Suddenly she sensed she was walk-

ing into a trap—why, she didn't know. But without even
having to think about it, she knew he was aware she hadn't
stayed in the hotel accommodation that had been reserved
for her. 'Er ... actually, I—er—didn't stay at the hotel.'
She watched as his eyes narrowed, and wished he wouldn't
look at her like that because it had the power to freeze her
brain and she needed to think up some excuse and fast.

'Oh?' His air was deliberately casual now, endorsing
her feeling that he had somehow discovered she hadn't
spent the night in the hotel.

'I have—er—an aunt living in London,' Gerry told him,
knowing she didn't have an aunt to her name, and must
be the world's worst liar. She had a feeling he knew she
was lying, but decided he couldn't very well challenge her
on the subject of her relatives. 'I'm staying with her while
I'm here.'

'And where in London does this *aunt* live?'

Oh lord, she didn't know London from Timbuktu.
'Finchley,' she said, forcing confidence into her voice as
the name dropped into her head—she was sure it was
somewhere near London, wasn't it? Hadn't she seen it on
the tube sticker?

Her relief was boundless when he dropped his questioning. 'You will have thought to cancel your hotel accommodation?' was all he said as he stood up intimating their
interview was over.

'I'll do it today,' she assured him, standing up at the
same time, feeling more confident now as some of her calm
returned.

As he came level with her she turned to face the door,
and when he went in front of her to open it, his back
towards her, she couldn't resist putting up her hands to
rub her tingling shoulders where his hands had crushed
them. She wasn't quick enough in dropping her hands to
her sides, and felt the faint pink of colour suffuse her
cheeks as he turned unexpectedly and caught her action.

She thought she saw remorse in his glance as his eyes found hers, but it was gone in an instant as she gave an embarrassed laugh and said with as much calm as she could muster:

'Remind me never to get pregnant—I'm sure you'd put me in plaster for a month if you had to find a new P.A. for your cousin!'

His eyebrows ascended that she knew William Hudson was his cousin, but he didn't comment on it; she would rather he had done so, rather than say what he chose to say, which had the power to deflate her completely. 'My dear Miss Barton,' he said coolly, 'P.A.s are two a penny.'

Gerry stalked out into the corridor ahead of him as with exaggeration he held the door open and almost bowed her out. Then he had overtaken her and she hated having to hurry after him, but could do nothing else if she wasn't to lose sight of him completely among the many doors and corridors in the building.

He didn't stay very long after introducing her to Janet Langley, though she did learn before he left her in Janet's charge that he would be out of town until Wednesday, and might not have the chance to see her again before she left for Little Layton. Thankful for small mercies, Gerry buckled down to learn everything Janet Langley had to teach her. Janet was a friendly girl with a curly mop of red hair, and only a few years older than herself. She had a bubbling-over manner when the two of them were together, but was crisp and efficient in her dealings over the telephone or when talking with clients in a way that greatly impressed Gerry.

For all she hadn't thought there would be very much difference in their two jobs, Gerry drove back to Little Layton on Monday night with her head buzzing with new impressions and ideas, and the knowledge that there was a lot more involved in the job of P.A. to a Company Secretary than Mr Gillett had shown her.

Teddy came out to greet her as she pulled the A35 on to the drive. She would have liked five minutes to unwind, but greeted her sister with warmth and affection and asked how her day had gone.

'Much better than I thought it would,' Teddy told her, obviously glad to see her back.

The return journey had taken longer than the journey to London earlier that day, and it was nine o'clock before Gerry was sitting down attempting to eat the meal that Teddy, true to her word, had made. On the way home she had thought she was ravenous, but now, with a plate of steaming casserole before her, her appetite left her. For Teddy's sake—after all, her day couldn't have been too easy coping with the twins—she made a brave stab at eating some of it, but had to give up half way through.

'That was delicious, Ted,' she said, pulling back from the table. 'Do you mind if I leave the rest—what I could do with now is a nice hot bath.'

For no reason she could think of, once she was in her bath, unexpected tears began to roll down her face, and she had to fight very hard to blink back further tears—she didn't even know why she was crying. It was a luxury she couldn't afford if she didn't want Teddy upset if she were to notice her red eyes. I'm overtired, I expect, she thought, dragging herself wearily out of the bath. A few hours' sleep and I'll feel as fit as a fiddle.

On Tuesday she was again at the London office with time to spare, only a few minutes this time, though, but at least she was there before nine. Only one more day to go and she could get back to her old routine. As she had suspected, all she'd needed was a few hours' sleep to put her right. The tiredness of last night had left her and what with Janet's bright personality, she felt quite enthusiastic as she was instructed further into the true nature of the job.

By lunch time she knew she was flagging, and blamed

her lack of energy on the fact that getting up at five in the morning was strictly for the birds. She forced herself to appear brighter than she felt, and was sure Janet had no idea how she was feeling when she remarked after she'd picked up something she was showing her in record time, 'Hey, I thought all the whiz-kids were kept in London!'

Half way towards Little Layton that night, Gerry just had to pull into a layby. It was no good—she had to have a five-minute break from driving. She'd felt quite dizzy a moment or two ago; she must be heading for a cold or something, she thought. While her mind argued she couldn't have a cold, not in a cottage as small as theirs—the twins would be sure to get it, and she didn't feel she had the energy to nurse them through it and possibly Teddy as well.

After ten minutes she began to feel better, and knowing Teddy would be anxiously looking out for her, she pulled out of the layby and carried on to Little Layton. Teddy didn't complain that she barely touched her meal, but Gerry saw her eyes go to her plate.

'It's the change in meal times, I expect,' Gerry said placatingly. 'My appetite will perk up once we're back to normal.'

'Only one more day!' Teddy exclaimed, looking forward to the last of the London trips as much as Gerry was.

The journey the next day followed the same pattern as the two previous mornings. And with her confidence growing Gerry neared London, a feeling of relief in her heart that tomorrow morning, the twins permitting, she could stay in bed until seven. She had no idea where she was when her offside tyre suddenly went flat. All she knew was that she was heading in the right direction having turned on to a main road ten minutes ago. She had another half an hour's driving in front of her and with a fair proportion of the working population roaring past her in their cars—gallantry that might be with them at a less pressing hour sorrowfully forgotten—it was not the most convenient time of the day to have a flat tyre.

There was nothing for it but to attempt to change the wheel herself. And a most frustrating job she was making of it, she thought, for after taking the spare wheel from the boot and deciding which end of the jack did what, she found the nuts holding the wheel to the car were too tightly fixed for her strength to undo. Refusing to be beaten, she made attempt after attempt to free them, and it was like music in her ears when a voice close at hand said:

'You look to be in a spot of bother. Do you want to leave it to an expert?'

Looking up, Gerry saw a man of about her own age had come to see what she was up to, and gratefully she handed over the tool she was holding, refusing to look at her now filthy hands. Her eyes strayed instead to the rear of her car and she saw that knight of the road had pulled in behind her in a very smart-looking sports car, only she had been concentrating so hard she hadn't heard him.

'Have far to go?' he asked, talking as he worked.

'Not far—about fifteen miles or so.'

'D'you think the old girl will make it?' he asked, giving the A35 a pat. 'I could drop you where you're going if you like.'

He could have been just being kind, he could have been trying to pick her up, but Gerry gave him a beaming smile as she refused his offer. For without wishing to conjure him up, a picture of Crawford Arrowsmith sprang into her mind—a picture of him saying she looked washed out. True, she hadn't had many male admirers lately and she knew she had only herself to blame for that—they were a luxury she just couldn't afford, Teddy needed her spare time more than anyone else—but if as she guessed the man who was now looking at her as if her smile had just knocked him off balance was in fact trying to pick her up, then she couldn't be looking as washed out as Crawford Arrow-smith had said.

The man straightened up and put the wheel he had just removed and the rest of the equipment back into the boot, and with his hand still on the boot lid enquired, 'You're sure I can't give you a lift?'

'No, thanks all the same. I'm sure the *old girl* won't let me down.'

'You wouldn't like to give me your phone number, I suppose?'

He had an engaging grin that somehow reminded her of Robin, for all he was nothing like Robin to look at, though for a moment she couldn't remember what Robin had looked like—which was strange, because she had thought herself very much in love with him.

'My time's fully committed,' she said. And because he was really very nice and had been very kind to her, she added, 'I'm sorry.'

'Beaten to the post yet again,' he said, his grin coming easily. 'Some fellows have all the luck!'

He passed her shortly afterwards—the A35 doing a sedate thirty—and gave her an uproarious burst from his horn. Gerry was still smiling over the encounter when she parked the car prior to haring to the tube station.

It was twenty-past nine when she hurried through the entrance of Arrowsmith Computers, and knowing she couldn't do a thing until she had washed some of the grime off her hands, she spent another five minutes in the cloak-room.

Walking quickly, she turned into the corridor that housed the door to the office she was sharing with Janet, and felt her heart fall to her feet as she saw Crawford Arrowsmith talking to another man a few doors up from Janet's office. Feeling very self-conscious, she walked on, knowing she would have to pass him to get to Janet's door. Not faltering in her stride, she composed her features and

wondered whether to give him a cool good morning or
totally ignore him. She decided on the latter, as he seemed
not to have seen her but was listening intently to what the
man with him was saying.

She was level with him when some of Crawford's reply
hit her ears, '... If you think that will work, Harry ...'
then almost past him, she felt her arm caught and held,
and felt herself being hauled back against Crawford's side,
then heard him continuing without any break in his conversation, and still looking as though he hadn't even seen
her—as if his hand had come out and stayed her progress
without his knowledge. 'I should do that,' he was saying
to the unknown Harry. Gerry jerked her arm to be free
and was ignored as he held on to her, and seethed quietly
as she was forced to stand waiting until he was ready to
give her his attention.

'Right, Mr Arrowsmith,' Harry said, 'I'll get on with
that straight away,' and with that he stepped smartly down
the corridor. He hadn't so much as looked at her, Gerry
thought, and couldn't help wondering if she had suddenly
become invisible.

Then Crawford was pulling her round until she was
standing directly in front of him. She was getting used to
the way he looked straight into her face by now, but it did
nothing for her rising temper to see he was again thinking
she looked washed out. She would dearly love to tell
him she could have been picked up that morning if she
had chosen, but didn't know that she felt up to any
reply he would have made to that.

'I see your aunt has a faulty alarm system too,' he stated,
her arm still in his grip.

She had to think fast to catch up with him, then remembered she had told him she was staying with her aunt
in Finchley, and he must be referring to her lateness, and
cancelling out her excuse before she made it that her aunt's
alarm had failed to go off. She knew she should apologise

and tell him she was sorry she was late—he had warned her in Layton about being late. It was important, she knew, for her to keep on the right side of him; her very future, hers and Teddy's, depended on his keeping her in his employment. But for once she felt she couldn't knuckle down to him. It was as if there was more at stake than the fact of her being late—somehow it seemed important that she didn't let him override her all the time.

'Will you let go of my arm?' she said coolly.

'And if I don't?'

She caught a gleam in his eyes and thought, damn him, he's enjoying this. Not taking her eyes off his, she stated simply and very calmly:

'If you don't, Mr Arrowsmith, it will give me the greatest pleasure to deliver one heartfelt kick to your shins.'

Whatever she expected, what happened next was the last thing she would have dreamed would have happened. For Crawford Arrowsmith, the head of the multi-million-pound combine, looked steadily at her for all of one second, then as a smile tugged at his mouth as though refusing to be restrained, he tipped back his head and a very pleasing laugh struck her unbelieving ears.

Amazement fought with wonder that her calmly voiced comment had struck at his sense of humour, and while she was still trying to comprehend the fact that she, Geraldine Barton, had actually made this rude, overbearing man laugh, the humour disappeared from his face and he was saying soberly, 'I knew the real you would have to come to the surface before too long.'

And then, while she was still trying to think up something sharp in reply to that, he was hauling her even closer to him, and she saw his head coming down to meet her, and knew herself powerless to stop him. She felt his lips close over her own and thought she was going to faint from sheer shock.

Then it was over and she might have imagined those

warm lips had ever claimed her own. She tore her trans-fixed gaze away from his mouth, all her energies busy try-ing to gather the security of a false calm about her.

'Perhaps, Miss Barton, I've hit on the one way of en-suring you are never again late arriving for work. I'm sure you gained as little pleasure from that—small punish-ment as I did.' With that he let go of her arm and strode past her.

She didn't look behind to see where he was going. Her own radar seemed decidedly faulty and she needed all her concentration to get her the remaining few steps down the corridor to the door of Janet's office.

Crawford had said he gained no pleasure from kissing her—well, she didn't doubt that; she already knew he had no liking for her. But what of her own feelings? Was she so starved of masculine caresses that even a kiss from that brute had seemed pleasurable? It wasn't that—she knew it wasn't. But she couldn't hope to argue against the voice inside her that yelled to be heard—she had felt the touch of his mouth against her own anything but as objectionable as she would have supposed. Unable to deal with such traitorous thoughts, she opened the door to Janet's office and went in.

Janet reminded her during the morning that it was her last day, and as they broke from their work for a few mo-ments, asked, 'Have you enjoyed your three days with us?'

Gerry hadn't stopped to wonder whether she had or not. As far as she was concerned it was one mad rush to get here, and another mad rush to get home to her sister. But the part in between, the actual time spent with Janet and seeing how she did things had been most instructive and—yes, now she came to think of it, most enjoyable.

'Do you know,' she said, trying to keep the surprise out of her voice, 'I rather think I have.'

'Good,' said Janet, seeming pleased. 'I think Mr Arrow-smith was concerned that you should be happy with us—

you'll be able to tell him he had nothing to worry about.'

Gerry couldn't quite see that Crawford Arrowsmith would be one whit bothered whether she was happy or not. Ever since that first day she had come into contact with him it seemed to her he had gone out of his way to make her feel miserable. That kiss hadn't been designed to cheer her up either. But she decided against telling Janet how wrong she was, and the two of them got down to discussing the remaining items Janet had left till last.

Back in Little Layton and in bed that night, Gerry tried to relax. Everything was now back to normal. She didn't have to get up at the crack of dawn in the morning and coax the A35 to London. With luck she should get another two hours' sleep. She felt tired enough to need it —didn't know when she had ever felt more tired—and yet sleep eluded her.

She looked across to the other bed, the beam of moonlight showing up Teddy's blonde head, turning her hair to wisps of silver as it spread over her pillow. Poor Teddy, she'd had an awful time. Was she right in thinking Teddy was starting to get over her grief at losing Mark? She hoped so.

Her thoughts drifted on to thoughts of Crawford Arrowsmith. She didn't want to think of him, would rather think of someone else, but he just wouldn't go away. She recalled the touch of his mouth, warm against her own. His kiss had been in no way passionate—but it hadn't been the sort of kiss one gave one's maiden aunt either. She turned silently in her bed as if to turn her back on thoughts of him, but that didn't keep him out of her mind. If it wasn't for fear of disturbing the twins, she'd go and make herself a warm drink, she thought, but even the action of movement was denied her, and she was forced to lie still and battle to oust Crawford Arrowsmith from her thoughts.

I must sleep with one ear cocked, she mused the next morning when Emma crying in the next room roused her

from sleep. She had lain awake ages last night and had no
idea what time it had been when sleep had finally claimed
her. Teddy was still sleeping solidly when she climbed out
of bed to go and quieten Emma. It was as well for Teddy
to have as much rest as she could, once her day started
there would be no stopping until she was able to put the
twins down for their nap.

'And what's the matter with you, young lady?' Gerry
whispered to the bright-eyed Emma.

Emma answered in what could have been Hindustani
for all the sense her aunt could make of it. But the way
she held up her arms to be picked up could not be mistaken. Gerry nursed her over her hip as she took her into
the kitchen and filled the kettle. Sarah, blonde like her
mother, was still asleep, and Emma was as sweet as a little
angel as she snuggled up to her dark-haired aunt.

'Why didn't you wake me?'

Gerry looked up to see a yawning Teddy in the door-
way. The tea was made and she had just poured two cups.
'I was going to bring you a cup,' she said in answer.

'Thank the Lord we're back to normal! If your boss has
any more bright ideas, tell him what he can do with them.'

Teddy's suggestion had infinite appeal, Gerry thought
as she drove into Layton. But with luck, he wouldn't have
any more bright ideas. Then suddenly thoughts of Crawford were forced to take a back seat, for the A35 began
to act strangely, and with a groan, and an exclamation of,
'Oh no—it can't be!' Gerry pulled into the side of the
road, quickly got out of the car, and saw she had a puncture. If she'd been the weeping sort, she thought, she
would have sat right down on the side of the kerb and
howled her eyes out—she felt defeated somehow, and experienced the same tired feeling that had beset her in the
bath on Monday night when she had given way to a few
tears without knowing it. Trying to pull herself together,

she stood and looked and looked at the offending tyre as if hoping by some magic the tyre would inflate itself and be all right again.

Now what am I going to do? she muttered. She had a spare wheel in the boot, certainly, but that was still flat from yesterday, there had been no time to have it fixed. She flicked a hurried glance at her watch. It had already gone ten to nine. If she left her car where it was and forgot about it until lunch time it would take her all of fifteen minutes to walk to the office. She wasted another two precious minutes in wondering what to do for the best—then deciding the car would come to no harm parked where it was, she set off, hurrying now, to get to Arrowsmiths, hoping against hope that Crawford was still in London. She would have to telephone a garage when she got to the office—her mind wouldn't cope with the question of how much their help was going to cost.

Even before she opened her office door she suspected the worst, and her heart sank as she saw through the communicating door that Crawford Arrowsmith was already seated behind his desk. Oh, why couldn't he still be in London?

Wasting no time, she popped her bag down by the side of her chair and began to look through her pending tray to see what if anything had been placed there. Her fingers hesitated as she became aware that Crawford had left his desk, and when she knew he had come to stand near her, was possibly watching her every movement, her fingers came to a halt and she was forced to look up at him. He was dressed in a light grey suit with a very fine check in it, and she couldn't help thinking how well it became him before she stepped on the thought and prepared herself for his acid comments.

'It would appear,' he said mildly, none of the acid she had been expecting evident in his tones, 'that since it is now,' he made a deliberate study of his watch, 'nine-fifteen precisely, you must take kindly to the penalty I issued when you were late yesterday.'

Hurriedly she turned her eyes away from him, and gripped hard at the edge of her desk. Very funny, she was sure! She was certain he had no intention of kissing her again, but felt herself go tense nevertheless. Then looking up again, she saw Crawford's eyes were doing a thorough search of her face. She knew she couldn't be looking washed out this morning, for her cheeks were still over-heated from her rush to get to the office. She was aware also that she had lost the prim look she adopted for the office. In her rush tendrils of hair had escaped from the confines of the tightly drawn back bun, but she had thought better than to waste more time by checking her appearance in the cloakroom. She watched Crawford's lips tighten as he studied her, and felt her composure slipping fast, and even though she made every effort to hold on to it, felt forced to blurt out:

'My car broke down.'

'What's the trouble? Or don't you know?' His voice was still mild, but she felt he was keeping it so only by a great effort.

'Puncture, I think.'

The energy she had expounded in reaching Arrow-smiths, albeit fifteen mintes late, seemed to have taken the stuffing out of her—she couldn't understand it, and thought again she might be going down with a cold.

'That's not much of a problem—won't take long to change the spare wheel over.'

'The spare is flat.'

Crawford looked as though he would like to tell her exactly what he thought about such negligence, but he restrained himself. 'Where did you leave your car?' he asked instead, adding, 'I'll get one of the mechanics to go and tow it in.'

Without thinking her pride was up in arms. She didn't want his help. She didn't want him doing anything for her that he could be sarcastic about at some future date.

'That's not necessary,' she said, becoming heated, even while an inner voice was telling her there was no need to get agitated over such a trifling matter. 'All I have to do is make a phone call.'

'I shouldn't think *dear Teddy* will like having to shift himself to come all this way to see to his mistress's car,' Crawford said cuttingly, having no idea Gerry was meaning to telephone a garage the minute he had returned to the other office.

As his words reached her ears, something within her exploded, and she didn't know who was the more surprised, herself or Crawford. For all the coolness, all the calm, the efficient surface she presented to anyone at Arrowsmiths who came into contact with her was dispersed without fight as an uncontrollable urge to take that sneering look off his face gave way to temper. Then several things happened at once.

'Shut up!' she yelled at him, and was on her feet as the words unrepentantly left her lips, feeling a glow of satisfaction that for however briefly, she had managed to astonish him. Her satisfaction was shortlived, as appalled by her lack of control, she gasped in horror as she realised Crawford would want retribution in full.

She was trembling even before his hands snaked out to take her by the arms. She knew at the very least he was going to shake the living daylights out of her, and her head swam with the enormity of what she had just done. To think she, Geraldine Barton, whose very livelihood depended on the mercy of the head of the Arrowsmith empire, had lost control so entirely as to almost scream at him to 'Shut up'! Numbly she shook her head as if to clear it, felt the presssure of those hands on her arms increase, and as though compelled lifted her head to gaze into slate grey eyes, that instead of being afire with fury as she would have supposed were looking at her in what she could only describe as concern. She knew she had mistaken that look, and turned her head away knowing she was going to have to apologise and hoping she would be allowed to do so and not be goaded into losing her temper again.

'I'm sorry, I shouldn't have ...' she began, and got no further, for the door leading from the corridor opened, and glad of the respite from the onslaught she knew Crawford was going to heap upon her head, she turned to see who had intruded on the holocaust that had been about to break.

And then her trembling started afresh, for as she barely felt Crawford's hands leave her arms, Gerry's eyes registered—while her mind refused to believe it—that the thinly built, tall man who had just come in was someone she had thought never to see again. For the man who had just entered the room was the man she had thought had transferred with his job to Birmingham, and he was the man she had fifteen months ago refused to marry.

CHAPTER FIVE

'ROBIN!' Gerry gasped, the unexpected sight of him blotting out for the moment the fact that Crawford had been just about to flatten her with a few well-chosen sentences, as she looked at the man she had been in love with what now seemed like a decade ago. Robin, she saw, was looking at her as if he couldn't quite believe she was the same girl he had been forced to part from. Gerry's mind registered this as she sought round for something that would loosen the tongue that seemed stuck to the roof of her mouth. She hadn't changed all that much though to deserve such an incredulous expression, surely? Admitted, she was about a stone lighter, and Robin would have remembered her with her hair in a different style—though, she conceded, if she looked as pale as she felt perhaps there was some justification for his stupefied look.

Robin didn't say her name as she had done his. Whatever he had been planning to say seemed to have disappeared completely as he stared at the girl he remembered as laughing-eyed, with her hair flowing freely to her shoulders in deep waves.

'My God!' seemed to be dragged from him. 'What's happened to you? You look ...' He hesitated as if stuck for words, and trying to recover from the shock of seeing him, Gerry thought, if he tells me I look washed out, I shall scream and scream and scream!

Then Crawford looked from one to the other, and put in quietly, 'You see a change in Miss Barton? How long is it since you've seen her?'

Gerry looked at Crawford then. The shock of seeing Robin had temporarily taken out of her mind that while she had been prepared to apologise for telling him to 'Shut up', she had known they had in truth been warming up to a full pitched battle. When Robin had so shatteringly walked through the door, he had caused their row to be suspended. She had no doubt it would start up again the moment Robin left—but meantime she had to give Crawford full marks for restraining himself while there was a third person present. But she did take exception to his attempting to discuss her as though she wasn't even there.

'I haven't seen Robin in over twelve months,' she stated flatly, feeling the need to make her presence known, and glad to find her vocal cords were still in working order.

Robin, it appeared, was still trying to connect the way she was now looking with the way in which he remembered her. 'Living with Teddy is doing you no good at all, in my opinion,' he said.

Which in Gerry's view was unforgivable, especially as he had come out with it in front of Crawford. Robin had never liked Teddy, though she couldn't think why other than that he might have been jealous of her at the time, but he'd had long enough to get over those feelings.

'I take it you know Miss Barton very well?' Crawford was asking, being intent, it seemed, on ignoring her. Intent, she thought, on finding out from Robin everything he could about her, though why he should be that interested she couldn't think, unless he wanted more ammunition to fire at her later.

'I know Gerry very well,' Robin was freely admitting, seeming to know without an introduction being performed that Crawford was a man of some power. 'In fact I thought at one time she was going to marry me.'

Gerry heard Robin's calmly voiced statement and felt the blood roaring in her ears. Was there no end to what he would tell a stranger at a first meeting? she wondered. Then she stopped wondering about anything at all, for the dizziness she had experienced earlier was coming over her again, and she needed all her will power and concentration to keep vertical. Then even that was not enough, for she felt the room begin to sway around her, and without knowing why her eyes tried to focus on Crawford, as though instinct was telling her he was the one who would help her. Then his face was swimming too, and she caught a glimpse of his tight-lipped expression and let go of the desk with one hand stretching out towards him in mute appeal for help—then blackness closed in, and she knew no more.

When Gerry came round she was lying flat on her back with her feet propped up on a couple of telephone directories. She had no idea how long she'd been out—it could have been minutes or only seconds, but as her silken lashes fluttered apart, she saw the face of Crawford Arrowsmith bending over her and closed her lids firmly together again. She could remember nothing of what had gone on before she fainted, but instinct was telling her to lie still until she had gathered sufficient strength to deal with anything Crawford cared to throw at her.

As the mists in her head began to clear, she remembered Robin had been in the room, and sat up quickly as that remembrance brought her to full consciousness, her eyes roving round the room to see there was no one else there except her and her overbearing employer. Her movement to rise to her feet was halted by Crawford.

'I shouldn't go anywhere in a hurry for the moment.'

His tones were quite kind, she thought, and she couldn't help wondering if she had not yet properly come round—she must be imagining that he would use such a tone to her.

'Where's Robin?' She accompanied her question with a definite movement to rise to her feet, and found Crawford's hands on her arms assisting her to her chair—she couldn't help but be grateful for his help, for her legs felt decidedly wobbly.

'Feeling better?' he asked when she was seated, ignoring her question as though she had never uttered it.

'Yes, thank you—I don't know how I came to do such a silly thing ...' she began, about to apologise to him for passing out on him when he broke in.

'That's exactly what we're going to find out.' She looked at him blankly, her mind not capable at that moment of keeping up with him. Crawford read her questioning look and enlightened her, 'I think it's about time you saw a doctor.'

'But I ...'

'I know—you told me you'd seen your doctor last week. He told you, I believe, that you were as well as could be expected.' She could hear the acid creeping into his voice

and knew she wasn't up to it if he was all set for a couple
of rounds with the gloves off—she wasn't in his weight
class just now, and realised with certainty that she never
would be. Then miraculously his voice softened, the acid
gone, and he was saying coaxingly as one might with a
small child, 'Yóu know, Geraldine, something will have to
be done about you. We can't have you fainting about the
place.'

The fact that he had called her by her first name was
not lost on her, but any surprise she might have felt was
superseded by the thought of what was behind his determination that she should see a doctor. She thought for
a moment or two before coming to her conclusion. So that
was it! He wasn't particularly concerned about her personally—not that he had any reason to be—but it irked her
that his sole reason for wanting her to go down to the
medical centre was that as head of Arrowsmiths, he wasn't
prepared to have one of his employees pass out without
having the cause investigated.

Raising her eyes, she looked at him. He was standing
near to her leaning the backs of his thighs against her desk
as he looked down and returned her glance.

'I suppose if I refuse to go along to the medical centre,
you'll have the doctor come up here to see me?' she said
wearily, wishing she had the strength to fight him but feeling as though she'd had the stuffing knocked out of her.

Rising to her feet, she was glad to find her legs were
stronger and more able to support her, while the wild
idea came to her of leaving the office and staying in the
cloakroom for fifteen minutes and then returning saying
the doctor had given her a clean bill of health. The more
the idea grew in her mind, the more she liked it.

'I'll go now,' she said, preparing to leave the office, and
was stopped when Crawford leaned down, picked up her
handbag and handed it to her. If he thought she had given
in very easily, it didn't show in his face, and though she

didn't need to take her handbag to the surgery, she thanked him just the same, and made for the door.

It was a little disconcerting to find him walking beside her before she was many yards down the corridor. She carried on walking, hoping he would revert to his normal stride which would have him turning the corner before she was anywhere near it—she hadn't the strength to hurry.

But it seemed Crawford wasn't in any hurry either. Unspeakingly he escorted her to the ground floor and kept close to her side until they came to the doors at the rear of the crowded car park. Good, she thought, when his steps slowed, he must be going out. All she had to do was to carry on walking, wait a few minutes round the corner, then, when she was sure he wouldn't be coming back, she could return to her office and he would never know she had been nowhere near the surgery.

But when they were level with the doors where they would part, she felt his hand take her elbow, and since she wasn't walking very quickly, felt herself being gently turned round to face him.

'This way,' he said quietly, the set of his face brooking no argument.

'But the surgery is that way,' she reminded him, pointing in the direction she had been walking. 'I thought you said I was to see the doctor.'

'That's true. You're going to—and good though Dr Butterworth is, I think we'd better have your own man take a look at you.'

'You mean . . .' Gerry felt waves of dizziness wash over her again, though this time it was caused more by the breathtaking high-handedness of the man than from any illness he imagined she was suffering from.

'I mean, Miss Barton, that I'm taking you home, and home you will stay until you're completely recovered.'

'This is ridiculous,' she argued, but there was no fire in her argument—she knew she was beaten, for all she tried hard. 'I'm perfectly well,' she protested, and couldn't think why she felt like bursting into tears.

'You look it,' Crawford told her edgily, almost pushing her through the doors and into the car park. 'You haven't a scrap of colour in your face, and if you weren't so screwed up with playing nursemaid to this fellow you live with you'd have done something about yourself long ago.'

She wanted to rail at him, to snap and fight, to stand her ground and tell him she wasn't going anywhere with him. His remarks about the 'fellow she lived with' washed over her head, even the thought of Teddy's shock when she saw her being brought home by her employer suddenly didn't seem to matter any more. She felt tired— wanted to give in to the feeling that was swamping her, the feeling that it was a relief to be looked after for a change. It was pure guilt at that thought that had her coming to a halt and looking up at Crawford as he stood, still with his hand on her elbow.

'I don't want to go home,' she almost whispered, her eyes misting over with the weakness of tears. 'Teddy will be upset.'

Crawford looked back at her, a spurt of fire flickering in his eyes at her words. Then covering any anger he might have been feeling, he urged her over to where his car was parked, permitting himself to say no more than a terse, 'Then I'm afraid *Teddy* will *damn well* have to *be* upset!'

It had been a mistake to close her eyes, Gerry thought as the car left Arrowsmith Electronics behind. The engine was positively purring and lulling her to sleep. There was no chance now, she knew, of reverting to the cool, calm P.A. she had tried to show Crawford she was, but she struggled against the soporific comfort of the car, determined to be sitting upright and not to alarm Teddy when they reached the cottage.

To get to Little Layton they had to drive along the route she had come along earlier that morning, and it was only when she saw her familiar cream-coloured A35 that she remembered about her puncture.

'My car,' she said, pointing it out as they passed it. 'I forgot all about it.'

'I'll have it attended to,' Crawford told her, his tone telling her not to argue. 'Give me your car keys.'

Meek as a lamb, and not understanding at all the ease with which she obeyed his command, Gerry fumbled round in her handbag and handed him the keys. I'll fight him tomorrow, she thought, for today, she was beginning to realise, she would have to give in to him. Her head had started to ache—she just wanted to be left alone.

When they arrived in Little Layton she directed him to the cottage and willed herself ready to summon up a smile when she saw Teddy—she'd have to get the strength from somewhere. She was sure Crawford would drop her off at the gate; there would be no need for Teddy to know she had fainted.

But for all her resolve her body was not quick enough to obey her when Crawford pulled up outside Honeysuckle Cottage, and he was round at her door, opening it and assisting her out before she could get further than putting her fingers over the door handle.

'Thank you for bringing me home,' she said, going through the gate and ready to close it behind her knowing he wouldn't be coming any further.

She found her gratitude totally ignored as he came through the gate with her and placed his hand once more beneath her elbow to escort her up the path. Gerry had a feeling that whatever she said, Crawford would do exactly as he pleased, so she wasted no further energy—she wasn't surprised when they reached the unlocked back door to find Crawford had followed her in.

There was no sign of Teddy when they went into the kitchen. Gerry circumnavigated the clothes horse that was propped up airing several nappies, and went through the living room to check, calling Teddy's name softly as she went. All was quiet—a sure sign Teddy was out. She'd probably taken the twins for a breath of fresh air, she surmised, and turned to go back into the kitchen to find Crawford staring as though mesmerised at the clothes horse and its contents.

'You have a child?'

He looked winded somehow, his voice sounding sharp and accusing in her ears. But before she could reply a dizziness she couldn't control washed over her and she clutched at the object nearest to her, which happened to be Crawford, glad to have the support of his hard body against her as she fell forward and rested for a brief moment until the world righted itself once more.

'I'm ... sorry,' she managed, hating that she was feeling weepy again. 'I ...'

She got no further, didn't even protest when a strong arm came beneath her legs and she felt herself hoisted aloft and held against him as, held securely, she was carried up the stairs that led off the kitchen and he went to investigate the rooms upstairs.

What he thought when he looked into the room that housed the two cots, complete with their Donald Duck and Mickey Mouse transfers, in the twins' room, she had no idea, for all she could do was lean her head weakly against him and be glad of his solid chest beneath it. Crawford closed the door to the twins' room and opened the door that led into the room she shared with Teddy.

'Which bed do you sleep in?' he asked, his voice sounding short, as though he was having some trouble in controlling his emotions.

Her imagination was taking off, she realised as she indicated the bed nearest the door. Why she should feel that small tingle of regret when his arms left her as he placed her gently down on the bed, she couldn't think.

'Can you manage to get into bed by yourself?'

Gerry hadn't got as far as thinking of actually getting into bed, though the idea had infinite appeal. Perhaps if she were to lie down for a while her head would stop its throbbing.

'My head hurts,' she confessed, which she had to admit was no sort of answer.

And in the midst of pain she felt his hands gentle in her hair as he removed the confining pins, muttering something that sounded like, 'It's likely to with your hair screwed back like that!' Her hair fell down about her shoulders, springing into the deep waves in joyous release, softening the look of her, making her seem vulnerable and untouched. She knew Crawford was looking at her. Even with her head pounding away, she was aware of a tenseness between them, but couldn't for the life of her look at him. And then his fingers were coming down to unbutton her blouse and she realised with a start of shock that he had every intention of helping her into bed.

Her fingers over his stayed his movement as he got to the second button. 'Please don't, Crawford,' she said, and in her agitation to stop him before he got any further, had no idea she had used his first name.

His hands fell away from her, and she looked up at him to see he was regarding her warmly, his eyes moving from her cloud of dark hair to her pain-filled wide brown eyes, to the opening of her blouse left by his own handiwork at the cleft of her breasts, and back to her face again. Then he was sitting on the bed beside her, his arm coming round her as he pulled her to rest her head against him.

'What's to be done with you?' he asked softly, and Gerry relaxed against him, needing his strength at that moment if she was ever to find the charge to top up her own diminished batteries.

A sound of someone moving about downstairs had her pushing away from him. Her movement was jerky and she caught the bedside table, causing the lamp it held to go crashing over on to the floor. She winced as the crash sent fresh pain thundering through her head, and Crawford left the bed to put the lamp to rights.

That sound downstairs could only mean Teddy was back. She would have heard the noise upstairs and would be panic-stricken thinking someone had broken in while she was out—for she would have realised by now that she had forgotten to lock the back door when she'd gone out.

Just as Gerry was pulling herself round out of the dreadful lethargy that was threatening to master her, knowing she would have to call Teddy's name and tell her she was home, she heard her sister's voice calling up the stairs.

'Who's that—who's up there?'

'It's me,' Gerry answered, and hoped Teddy could hear, for her voice sounded far off even to her own ears. 'I've come home early,' she added, forcing strength into her voice.

Immediately Teddy started up the stairs, and in seconds she was in the room, her eyes flicking to her sister and then growing wide as she saw the tall man who had been standing watching the door.

'Who are you?' she asked bluntly, her eyes going from him to Gerry and back again.

'Crawford Arrowsmith,' he supplied. 'Might I know who you are?'

Gerry tensed in the pause that followed. She saw comprehension dawn in Teddy's eyes as it came to her that the man who was half filling the room was his sister's employer. Gerry closed her eyes when her sister began to speak, acknowledging at last that she felt too ill to care that her cover was about to be blown.

'I'm Teddy,' she heard her say as if from a long way off. 'I'm Gerry's twin.'

Quite what made her groan the way she did, Gerry wasn't sure. Probably half because of the astounded look of Crawford's expression before she dropped her eyes away from him, and probably half because if she didn't soon lie down she was fairly certain she would fall down, she thought.

Her groan brought two pairs of eyes swivelling round to her, and while Teddy was gasping, 'Gerry?' as if unable to comprehend all was not right with her, Crawford was telling her sharply:

'Your sister is ill. Give me the phone number of your doctor, and get her into bed quickly!'

As though in a trance Teddy stared at him. Then, glad that someone was taking charge of the situation, she automatically answered the authority in his voice and told him Dr Bidley's number. Then, all her thoughts for her sister, she turned to Gerry as Crawford left the room.

'You do look peaky, love,' she admitted as she approached the bed. 'Come on, let's get you between the covers before your boss gets back.'

Teddy, Gerry discovered, could be efficient when she chose, and in no time had her tucked up in bed and was sitting beside her asking, 'What happened? You were all right when you left here this morning.' And before Gerry could say anything to reassure her—though to say anything, she felt, would be an effort—the door opened and without knocking and waiting in case she was still in a state of semi-undress, Crawford came in.

'Geraldine was far from all right this morning,' he answered for her. 'In fact I would go as far as to say she hasn't been feeling well for many a long morning.'

Gerry looked from one to the other. The tight-lipped look she was beginning to know had returned to his mouth, and even though she wanted to yell at him, to scream at him not to take his bad temper out on Teddy, to yell at him that Teddy wasn't as strong as she looked—she couldn't find the energy to enter into a row with him.

'But,' Teddy was saying, seeming unable to believe him, 'Gerry's never ill.' And as though the implication of her sister being ill had just hit her. 'She can't be ill, we need ...' She broke off as it came to her for the first time that she might be appearing to be a little selfish in front of this stranger who knew nothing, if she knew Gerry, of their circumstances. 'Did you manage to contact the doctor?' She thought better than to carry on with what she had been about to say. Gerry's boss was looking like thunder—so much so, she thought it cost him an effort to answer her at all.

'He'll be here before too long,' he told her shortly. Then looking over at Gerry who had watched, her eyes going from Teddy to Crawford, and who was now looking at him in silent appeal for him not to upset Teddy, his thunderous expression cleared, and he asked, 'How's the head?'

'Fine,' she lied huskily, and wished they would leave her so she could close her eyes. She felt so tired—she might even drop off to sleep if she was on her own now.

'You're dead but you won't lie down, will you?' said Crawford, and if she hadn't been feeling so dreadful, she would have thought he had a deal of charm about him as he said it. Which just went to prove, she thought, as she turned her head away, that Crawford was right and she wasn't at all well.

Paul Meadows arrived without her being aware he had negotiated the stairs. He was in the room, giving a quick glance to Teddy who was now standing at the bottom of the bed, before he looked past her and at the recumbent form of Gerry.

'You're the culprit, are you?' he said, brushing past Teddy and coming to sit beside Gerry on the bed. She thought he looked as pale as she felt, but he seemed quite cheerful as he went on with a charming bedside manner, 'I received a message about someone being ill at Honeysuckle Cottage—when I saw the twins sleeping like tops outside in their pushchair, I thought it might be your sister.'

Gerry looked away, feeling she ought to apologise for being ill—it wasn't any of her doing that he had come racing round to the cottage. But when she looked at him again, she saw his eyes were twinkling and she must have imagined his pallor, because he looked all right again now.

'I advised you to take care of yourself, Miss Barton,' he said, picking up her wrist and finding her pulse with the ease of one who does it every day. 'Though I must admit I didn't expect you to take any notice.'

'You advised her . . .' All eyes turned to Crawford as the impatient exclamation left his lips, and while they looked he seemed suddenly to grow fed up with the whole lot of them. 'I'll wait downstairs,' he said, making for the door, turning to ignore everyone but the doctor. 'I'd appreciate a word with you after you've examined Miss Barton.'

'Who was that?' Paul Meadows exclaimed after Crawford had disappeared. 'Your fiancé?'

'No,' Gerry gasped, feeling amusement stirring within her for the first time that day at the very idea. 'He's Crawford Arrowsmith, my boss.'

Whatever Paul Meadows thought his face remained bland, and he proceeded to examine her, while Teddy stood looking anxiously on. When he told her the result of his examination, both girls looked at him with shock.

'You're thoroughly exhausted,' he said quietly, putting away his stethoscope and taking out his prescription pad. 'What you need is complete rest and quiet.'

'Exhausted?' Teddy echoed, her eyes filling up with sudden tears.

'I'll be fine tomorrow, Ted,' Gerry assured her, being the first to recover, though badly wanting to close her eyes. 'All I need is a few hours' sleep, then I'll be as right as ninepence.'

'You will stay in bed for more than one day,' Paul Meadows said severely. 'I'll call in again tomorrow, and if

I catch you out of bed I shall make it my business to have you hospitalised.'

He was joking, was Gerry's initial reaction, but to her horror, before she could think further, she burst into tears. And what was worse, once she had started to cry she didn't seem able to stop. Vaguely she was aware of a conversation going on between Teddy and the doctor, then Teddy was coming over to her and crying with her, then Paul was taking her arm and she barely felt the prick of the hypodermic he plunged into her arm. Then blissfully—floatingly—the sleep she had yearned for was about her, and she drifted off into a fairytale land where nothing mattered and she didn't have to fight people like Crawford Arrowsmith who were set on finding out her weaknesses.

For three days Gerry drifted between sleep and a twilight world. She didn't feel ill, just pleasantly drowsy. Every time she woke up, Teddy was there, and would each time pop a couple of tablets into her mouth which she would swallow and drift off into sleep again. Once she'd thought Crawford Arrowsmith had been there, but that part must belong to some dream she'd had while sleeping, she reasoned.

On the fourth day she awoke and didn't feel like going to sleep again. She felt better and ready to get up and continue living again. She must have eaten since she'd been in bed, but had no recollection of it, and now she was decidedly hungry. There were no sounds coming from downstairs, so she surmised that Teddy must have taken the twins out.

In a mind to go downstairs and get herself a bowl of cornflakes, she pushed back the covers and without thinking went to stand as had always come naturally to her, and received the shock of her life when her legs refused to hold her and she hit the floor with a bang.

She was still sitting on the floor in a dazed state, trying

to comprehend what had happened, when the door burst open and as she looked up, her eyes revealing her incomprehension at what had happened, the tall figure of Crawford Arrowsmith came into her line of vision.

He didn't waste time with words, but scooped her up as though she was one of the twins and held her while she gazed up at him.

'I fell over,' she said, thinking how stupid that sounded, when what she really meant to ask—no, demand—was what he was doing in the cottage.

She should be finding out where Teddy was. Surely Teddy wouldn't have gone out and left him alone in the cottage save for herself asleep upstairs? But none of these questions were voiced. And strangely, as she looked at him, it didn't seem to matter very much whether Teddy had gone out and left her alone with him. Which made her begin to wonder how ill she had been, because surely it wasn't right that she should feel so lightheaded.

'I'm not surprised you fell over if you've been trying to get out of bed.'

'I've always managed to get out of bed before without falling over,' she said in a bemused kind of way while she looked into his slate grey eyes, and wanting to giggle at the idiocy of what she'd said.

Crawford didn't seem to think she was being idiotic, though, and gave her a smile she found herself liking. 'I expect you still have your head half full of the tablets Meadows prescribed,' he explained. 'That plus the fact that three days in bed are not conducive to any athletics you might care to perform.'

'Three days?' She stared at him, her head clearing rapidly at the shock of knowing she had been in bed for such a length of time.

'Today makes four,' Crawford said matter-of-factly, and at that moment Gerry became aware of him as her employer.

Became aware she was dressed in a scanty nightie, which although covering her, had slipped up past her knees crooked over his arm. Became aware that her own arm was hooked around the back of his neck, and came vividly alive as a searing blush stained her face.

'I ... I ...' she began, and received the surprise of her life when Crawford dipped his head and kissed the tip of her nose.

'Couldn't resist that,' he said, moving towards the bed. 'You blush so prettily.' And without more ado he lowered her gently down and pulled the covers up over her. 'Feel like sitting up for a while?'

Gerry nodded, dumbstruck. Then feeling she ought to say something, if only to prove that she still could, she muttered, 'Yes, please,' and felt herself pulled gently up to lean against his chest for a brief moment while he adjusted her pillows.

'What were you out of bed for anyway?' he asked, as he took the chair from across the room and came to sit beside her.

'I felt hungry—I thought I'd go and ...'

'That's a sure sign you're getting better,' Crawford said easily. 'What do you fancy?'

Gerry looked at him and had a funny feeling deep inside her. From the look of him it would appear she had only to say what she would like to eat and he would go and get it for her. And that caused her to have the hardest work in the world in trying to remember he was her boss.

'I was going to get myself a bowl of cornflakes,' she said, trying to quieten the unknown feeling inside her.

'It's four o'clock in the afternoon,' he informed her, 'but if that's what takes your fancy ...'

'Afternoon? I thought it was still morning ...'

She found she was talking to the air, as Crawford left the room without another word. If he had gone to fetch her

her afternoon breakfast, he would never find anything, she thought, picturing him moving everything in the pantry looking for the cereal box. But in less than a few minutes he was back in the room carrying a tray which bore a long glass of delicious-looking milk, and the bowl of cornflakes she had requested.

She eyed the milk longingly—Crawford couldn't know of the economies she practised, and it wouldn't dawn on him, she thought, to think of making sure there was milk to see them through until the morning.

'Drink it up,' he told her, seeing her hovering with the glass in her hand. 'You look as though you can hardly wait —and I promise not to see if you dribble it down your chin.'

This teasing side of Crawford was certainly a side she had never seen before, had never imagined existed. But it eased any of the tension she had been beginning to feel, and made it comparatively easy to say, 'I don't think I'd better—the milkman isn't very reliable,' she hoped the milkman would forgive her because you could tell the time by him most days, 'and the twins will want some milk for their breakfasts.'

It was the first time she'd said anything ever about the twins, and she felt Crawford's hard look on her as her fingers left the glass to fidget with the top sheet. It was a mistake to look at him then, but she felt as though compelled, and she saw in his eyes a look that held a world of meaning. A look that said when she was more able, he had a few words he wanted to say to her on the subject of not only the twins, but also about the way she had let him think what he had about Teddy.

She found the top sheet quite fascinating—or so it would appear as her eyes hurriedly left his to stare down again. The silence lengthened between them and she felt the discomfort of tension spring up within her once more.

Then Crawford was staying the restive movements of her fingers and picking up her hand, forcing her to spread her fingers back round the glass.

'Drink it up,' he ordered, and when her mouth would have formed a stubborn line, 'There are five pints more in the fridge.'

Obediently Gerry took the glass from the tray. She had to believe what he said about the amount of milk in the fridge, because her legs hadn't the strength to take her down to the kitchen to investigate for herself. And anyway, she had an idea she was going to need all her reserves of strength, for as she put the glass back on the tray after taking a very satisfactory swallow, her eyes met Crawford's and she discerned a look in those slate grey eyes that was both severe and frosty, and she knew without being told that when she was well enough, he was going to say a few harsh and pertinent things to her.

CHAPTER SIX

THERE were more surprises in store for Gerry than she would have dreamed of the next day when she refused to stay in bed any longer. It was about eleven in the morning when she decided, while having to admit perhaps she had been a bit under the weather, that she was perfectly well now, and nothing was going to keep her in bed. She could hear movement going on downstairs, Teddy must be chasing round like a wild thing to cope with the housework and the twins, and a perfectly fit sister upstairs on whom she was waiting hand and foot.

Cautiously she began to get out of bed, conceding as

it took a few moments for her legs to obey her that she might perhaps qualify that perfectly fit to *almost* perfectly fit. Shrugging into her dressing gown and with the help of the end of the bed, she began to make her way downstairs. It was a slower business than she had been prepared for, but with a couple of rests on the way, she made it to the bottom of the stairs and paused to straighten up, ready to say she felt fine if Teddy was in the kitchen and had any idea of telling her to go back to bed.

There was no sign of Teddy as she entered a kitchen she barely recognised. Gone was the clothes horse that always decorated the room. There was not a dish in sight —nothing on the draining boards of the sink—even the bread board had been put away. Feeling slightly as though she had wandered into someone else's house, Gerry made her way slowly through to the living room. At the very least she expected to see some of the twin's toys or clothing strewn over the settee, but everywhere was immaculate. Then just as she was about to begin calling for Teddy, though commonsense had told her she must be out, the back door opened and she turned to see a wiry-looking lady of about fifty come into the kitchen, clad in a blue and white checked overall, and holding a duster in her hand.

'What are you doing down?' the woman asked, coming into the living room before Gerry could formulate the question and ask who she was. Then the woman was taking over completely, and saying, 'Come on, Miss Barton, let's get you sat down before you fall down.' Which was so much like something Crawford Arrowsmith had once said to her that Gerry's tongue stayed firmly still as she allowed herself to be helped over to the settee.

As she felt the solid comfort of the settee beneath her, Gerry's astonishment quickly evaporated, and she was able to ask, 'Who are you?'

'Didn't they tell you?'

Gerry had no idea who 'they' were, but she felt strong enough now to find out. 'They?'

'Mr Arrowsmith and Mrs Wilson,' the lady said as if that was all the explanation Gerry needed. Then seeing from her expression, the way her face had grown severe at the mention of Mr Arrowsmith's name, she went on, 'Well, it was Mr Arrowsmith really, I suppose—I'm Mrs Chapman, by the way. Well, I put a notice in the post office window saying I was available for babysitting—my own little ones are bigger than me now, and with Charlie gone—Charlie was my husband,' she explained, and although her face didn't show by a flicker of a muscle how much Charlie had meant to her, Gerry could tell from the way she said his name that he had been someone very special to her.

She wondered inconsequently if she would ever find someone very special in her life—she thought briefly of Robin, and knew with sudden clarity that Robin hadn't been that person, and didn't stop to think how she knew, when at one time she had thought he was everything she wanted out of life. Then she put these thoughts from her. She had no business thinking about anyone, special or not. Teddy would need her support for a good many years to come.

Mrs Chapman was absentmindedly rubbing her duster backwards and forwards across the mantelpiece as if she couldn't bear inactivity of any kind, and went on with what she had been saying. 'Anyway, Mr Arrowsmith came to see me about the babysitting, and asked if I knew anyone who could give a hand with some housework. Well, I liked the look of him,' Gerry stifled her surprise at this busy little woman taking to Crawford on sight—her own reaction had been very different, 'so I told him I could come for a few mornings a week and would come and keep an eye on the twins at the same time, and fill in on the occasional evening when you and your sister go out.'

Gerry tried to quell the panic that was growing within her as the implication of what Mrs Chapman was saying hit her. That she and Teddy never went out in the evenings was neither here nor there, but the colossal cheek of Crawford Arrowsmith to take it into his head to see they had some hired help was making her so angry she felt she would burst a blood vessel. She had to exert a great deal of control in order that Mrs Chapman should have no idea how her news had affected her. Then Mrs Chapman was asking, 'Shall I make you a nice cup of coffee?' and waited only for Gerry's smile of acceptance of a cup of the only luxury they allowed themselves before she trotted off to the kitchen.

The noise of Mrs Chapman busy in the kitchen faded into the background as Gerry tried to come to terms with the problem she had just been presented with. Crawford Arrowsmith could have no idea of how far she had to make her salary stretch. Apart from the first priority of finding the rent each month, there was the ever-present nightmare of the daily household expenses—the twins were growing at an alarming rate, and while she was glad about that, it seemed they needed something new every other week. Any time now their cots would have to be exchanged for a couple of beds—where the money was going to come from she hadn't yet been able to work out. And now, on top of that, she somehow had to find the money to pay for Mrs Chapman's services. She shook her head as though to scatter her depressing thoughts, wondering how she could tell this lady who was now handing her a cup of coffee—coffee, if she was not mistaken, made with all milk—that after today they would be able to manage on their own.

'Aren't you having a cup?' she asked, thanking her for the coffee and inviting her to sit down for a moment, though not looking forward to the coming interview. It annoyed her that she was the one to have to tell the willing Mrs Chapman that she was no longer needed. Crawford had been the one to hire her, he should be the one to fire her—not that he would be calling here again, but . . .

'I never drink coffee,' Mrs Chapman broke in on her thoughts. 'I had a cup of tea half an hour ago. I didn't bring you one up because Mrs Wilson said you had to drink as much milk as we could get down you.'

From which Gerry gathered there seemed a campaign afoot to get her fattened up. She ran a nervous hand over the back of her neck, bringing her fingers round unconsciously to touch the fine area of her collarbone. Perhaps she didn't have too much flesh on her bones at that. But it was difficult to adjust to being the one who needed looking after—and she didn't feel she could take very kindly to it.

'I won't sit down, thank you, Miss Barton.' Mrs Chapman picked up the duster she had left on the mantelpiece when she'd gone to make the coffee. 'Since you're down, I'll pop upstairs and tidy round.' And before Gerry could summon her back, she heard her going up the stairs.

Gerry wasn't left on her own for long enough to think very clearly what she was going to say to Mrs Chapman when she came downstairs again. For within a few minutes of her disappearance she heard the squeak of the twins' pushchair—she must get round to giving it a squirt of oil, she was thinking—then Teddy was coming breezily through the kitchen and exclaiming on seeing Gerry downstairs on the settee.

'I knew it!' she said, and Gerry was struck by how lighthearted Teddy was as she came into the room, and couldn't help but feel sad that if the cause of Teddy's new lightheartedness was because they had some help in the cottage, she was going to have to take that cause away. 'I knew the minute my back was turned you'd be out of that bed. How are you feeling?'

'Mrs Chapman's upstairs,' Gerry began without preliminaries, wanting to get what she had to say over and done with quickly—she knew Teddy wasn't going to like it.

'Oh, you've met her—she's a marvel, isn't she?' Teddy seemed completely unconcerned with regard to where they were going to get the money from to pay her, and looked round the room with a smile of content on her face. 'I bet you didn't recognise this room when you came down —she's even ...'

'Teddy,' Gerry broke in, and felt like weeping for what she was about to do to her sister. Teddy had been marvellous to her while she had been in bed—though she couldn't remember too much about it—but Teddy had seemed to be there whenever she awoke, apart from that one time when she'd dreamed Crawford had been there. She stamped down determinedly on all thoughts but the matter which had to be discussed. 'Teddy,' she said again, feeling a helplessness suddenly that was alien to her, 'we can't keep Mrs Chapman, you know.'

'We can't ...' She had Teddy's full attention now, and hoped Teddy wouldn't be too upset. She didn't feel up to coping with Teddy in tears just now. 'Why can't we?' Teddy asked quietly.

'We simply can't afford her.' Gerry gave her what she thought was a very valid reason, and was amazed when Teddy took on the elder sister role and patted her arm placatorily.

'Oh, if that's your only reason forget it,' she said soothingly.

Gerry didn't know how Teddy could be so lacking in understanding, and thought perhaps she should have told her more of how far the money had to go; her only reason for not doing so had been because to know they were living almost on the breadline would have done nothing for the little confidence Teddy had. But here was Teddy calmly telling her to 'forget it', and she didn't know how she was going to get through to her that Mrs Chapman was a luxury they just couldn't afford.

'I can't forget it, Ted,' she said gently. 'Mrs Chapman's wages ...'

'Crawford's paying,' Teddy cut in to her utter amazement—the way Teddy had so easily brought out his first name causing her to wonder how well the two of them had got to know each other while she had lain in bed.

'Crawford?' she repeated, aghast. 'Crawford Arrowsmith, you mean?'

'He's the only Crawford I know,' said Teddy, beginning to look slightly uncomfortable at her sister's staggered expression. Then gaining confidence, 'Don't worry, Gerry, it's all right.' She was back to being soothing again. 'When you were taken ill it was obvious I wasn't going to be able to cope on my own, and with Paul Meadows talking of sending you to hospital, and me feeling I'd be in the next bed with you if he did, Crawford took complete charge.' She looked at Gerry to see how she was taking it—not very well, she saw. 'Don't get all uptight, love,' she coaxed. 'Crawford and Paul Meadows will have my hide if you have a relapse—you shouldn't really be out of bed as it is.'

'But, Teddy ...' Gerry began helplessly, and saw Teddy's mouth take on a stubborn line which she knew from experience meant she was going to clam up any moment at all now, and there would be no talking to her for hours.

'Look, Gerry,' Teddy said with a severity Gerry wasn't used to seeing in her sister, 'we needed help—and fast. Crawford supplied it—I know it goes against the grain for you to accept anybody's help, but it doesn't go against mine. Life has played some dirty tricks on me, and if somebody wants to give me a hand to ease a dull monotonous day—there's no way I'm going to refuse it.' Her expression softened as she looked at Gerry's unhappy face, and she put her hand on her arm, saying earnestly, 'Forget your pride for once, love—Crawford was only trying to help. And anyway,' she added, the gentle moment gone, 'we need Mrs Chapman, and if you don't like that Crawford is paying her wages, take it up with him.'

Gerry knew she would take it up with him anyway—and pay him back the amount he had already paid Mrs Chapman. When she felt more up to it she would work out their budget again. Perhaps there was some economy she had missed—perhaps they would be able to afford Mrs Chapman for say two mornings a week. She doubted there was any economy they could make that they weren't already making, she thought with a sinking heart. Even when she was well enough to take her own share in the household chores, she had a feeling Teddy would still want Mrs Chapman's services during the daytime.

'I'll see him as soon as I get back to the office,' she told Teddy quietly.

'You'll see him before that, I expect,' said Teddy knowledgeably.

'Oh.' She wondered what Teddy knew that she didn't know, and wasn't very long in being enlightened.

'He's been here every day since you were taken ill.'

'He hasn't?' Gerry contradicted questioningly.

'He has,' Teddy affirmed, wondering why she hadn't thought to mention it earlier since it had satisfactorily got her sister off the subject of Mrs Chapman.

'What for?' Gerry asked, shaken that a man of Crawford Arrowsmith's importance should visit their tiny cottage every day. It just didn't seem likely that he could be that interested in the health of one of his P.A.s. 'He's not ...' she paused, and after a long moment brought out the thought that had come to her and which she didn't like at all, though she couldn't have said why, other than that it gave her a funny feeling deep inside to think of it.

'He's not—interested in you, is he?' she brought out at last, and was surprised at the relief she felt when Teddy laughed.

'No, you chump—honestly, the ideas you get! I should think I'd be the last person he'd be interested in—— Don't think he thinks much of me.' That makes two of us he doesn't think much of, Gerry thought, then Teddy went on, 'Well, perhaps that's a bit of an exaggeration. He was all snappy and snarly when he brought you home—then when he called the next day to see if you were any better ...'

'He didn't come upstairs, did he?' Gerry couldn't stop the question that rushed to her lips.

'Of course he did. Can you imagine a man of his type, after having put himself out to call, going away without seeing for himself how you were progressing?'

Gerry had to admit she couldn't, and knew now that the time she had dreamed of him bending over her had been no dream at all. Whatever was in those tablets Paul Meadows had prescribed for her had certainly done the work they were intended to do, though, for she had drifted off into sleep with only her subconscious registering that Crawford was there. And she knew for a certainty she would never have slept had she been fully aware he had been in her room. Never, while fully awake, would she allow her guard to slip in his presence. A memory of the way she had rested her head against him when he had sat with her on the bed after he'd driven her home flitted through her head, only to be pushed firmly away; she didn't want to remember that moment of weakness.

'You were saying,' she reminded Teddy, 'that you think I'll see him before I get back to the office. Do you think he'll call today?'

'Wouldn't be at all surprised if he didn't call tonight,' Teddy was saying when one of the twins outside decided to make herself heard.

Instantly Gerry forgot about everything else as Teddy went through the living room door. 'Bring them in to me, Ted,' she called after her. 'It seems ages since I last saw them.'

Emma and Sarah seemed equally as pleased to see their aunt as she was to see them, and gurgled happily one either side of her on the settee, as she placed an arm around each of them. Then Mrs Chapman was coming downstairs, and Gerry knew as the lady pulled her jacket on, on top of her overall, that the moment to have a quiet word with her had gone. Perhaps it was just as well, she reasoned, as she bade Mrs Chapman goodbye. After she had done her budget she might be able to ask her to come one day a week less. But whichever way her budget worked out, she was sure of one thing—Crawford Arrowsmith was not going to pay for their domestic help.

Gerry enjoyed being downstairs again, enjoyed once more being part of a family unit. Teddy wouldn't allow her to stir off the settee while she prepared a very substantial lunch, and Gerry ate as much as she could so as not to let Teddy's efforts go to waste, but she made a poor showing of an appetite.

'I probably don't need very much since I'm not expending any energy,' she told Teddy when she remonstrated with her.

'Paul Meadows says he wants to see you weigh seven pounds extra by the time the month is out,' Teddy told her. And something in the way she said Paul Meadows' name had Gerry looking up at her as she cleared the table, though Teddy didn't notice as she warmed to her theme. 'Honestly, Gerry, I had no idea you were so low—I feel dreadful that I was so wrapped up in my own problems that I didn't see you were fading away under my eyes.'

Gerry burst out laughing at that dramatic statement—she couldn't help it, for all Teddy was looking very serious.

'Fading away!' she scoffed. 'Really, Ted, that's exaggerating a bit, isn't it?'

'It's all very well for you to laugh,' Teddy said, seeing nothing funny in what she had said. 'Besides receiving a nasty shock at finding you home early with a big hunk of man in the bedroom—first I had Crawford giving me one hell of a bad time, then Paul was giving me what for because I hadn't noticed you were ill.'

Gerry didn't feel like laughing at that—all her concern was for Teddy, who wasn't used to the abrasive quality of Crawford's remarks. She was somewhat surprised, though, to hear that Paul Meadows had added his two-pennyworth when Crawford had finished.

'Well, you can forget about them now,' she said gently. 'I'll be back on my feet in no time, and there'll be no need for you to see either of them again ...' She paused as she recalled that Paul Meadows would be their doctor until Dr Bidley came back. 'Well, I shall take care of Crawford Arrowsmith,' she amended, showing Teddy a confidence she wasn't feeling. 'And with any luck, neither you nor the twins will need medical treatment before Dr Bidley comes back.'

'I might have to see him for the twins,' Teddy murmured, 'though it's to be hoped I won't. But I have taken my name off his list.'

'You haven't?' Gerry challenged. 'But why? He ...'

'Oh, I got into a temper the day he laid into me, and applied to be put on Dr Farraday's books in Middle Compton,' Teddy told her, naming a doctor who practised in the next village. 'I've kept the twins on Paul Meadows' register in case I need someone in a hurry.' Then she confessed, looking slightly embarrassed, 'I felt rather stupid about it after I'd done it—especially after I'd made a point of telling Paul Meadows what I'd done.'

'What did he say?' Gerry asked, interested.

'Not very much—just gave me a long look I couldn't

understand, then for the first time ever he smiled at me, and said, "If you hadn't taken that action, Mrs Wilson, I would have taken precisely those steps myself". D'you know, Gerry, I still can't understand why he doesn't want me on his register—I'm not as bad as all that, am I?'

'Of course you're not—he's probably realised he's got a few too many patients on his work load. You remember the job we had getting fixed up with Dr Bidley when we moved here. It was fortunate, though, that Dr Farraday could take you.'

They talked some more, and the afternoon wore on with the twins peacefully asleep upstairs. 'Do you think you ought to go back to bed now?' Teddy suggested after deciding it was time she had a look at Emma and Sarah. 'You can't be feeling anything like up to scratch yet, and Paul Meadows will be sure to think it's my fault it you take a retrograde step.'

Gerry didn't admit to Teddy how much the thought of getting back into bed appealed, but conceded, 'What I'd really like is a bath—I could bathe now, couldn't I, have a rest afterwards, and be up again in case Crawford Arrowsmith calls as you seem to think he will.'

Teddy helped her into the bath, instructing her to yell out if she felt faint, then went to take a look at her daughters.

It was delicious to lie there and have time to soak. Time to let thoughts come and go as they pleased. Gerry had time to think how well Teddy was coping in this, what she would have thought of at one time as a crisis. Had she got Teddy all wrong? She seemed to be coping marvellously —she had Mrs Chapman to help, of course. Gerry hurried over thoughts of Mrs Chapman, and the necessity to have words with Crawford about her, and determinedly turned her thoughts back to Teddy. Had her affection for her twin blinded her to stronger qualities in her she had never seen? She didn't think so—remembering the way she had sat and cried and cried when Mark had died—the way she had seemed all set to cave in when they had discovered he had died leaving her penniless. Gerry remembered still the utter hopelessness in Teddy's face—six months pregnant and in the depths of despair.

At first she had thought to seek Robin's help and advice. She had started to tell him when he'd called at the large house her father rented in Gringham. She had been so sure, she recalled, that Robin would know what they could do to help Teddy, but before she had got very far he had said quite bluntly, his voice she had thought at the time totally devoid of sympathy, 'Teddy's in one hell of a mess, isn't she?' and that had been all the interest he had shown in her plight, for he had gone on then to talk of his pending transfer within the accountancy firm he worked for to Birmingham. She hadn't wanted to leave their talk of Teddy there—sure in her own mind Robin would be able to come up with some suggestion that would help Teddy. But she had listened to him talk about how things were moving for him, how once he got to Birmingham it would be only a short step before he was promoted to a managerial position, and then he was asking her to go with him, asking the question she had been hoping for weeks he would ask, for they had already talked of their love for each other, though nothing had been said about marriage, and she had begun to wonder if their relationship would continue in the static role that had seemed likely. 'Marry me, Gerry,' he'd said. And she had forgotten Teddy long enough to enjoy the embrace that had followed, as they had kissed.

They had broken away from each other at last, and she had looked at him starry-eyed. Had been on the verge of telling him what he had known all along—that he only had to ask and she would marry him and go anywhere in the world with him. But before the words could leave her lips, a picture of Teddy, now sedated and in bed upstairs, sprang up in front of her.

'But what about Teddy?' Happy in her own love for Robin, she had just been waiting, as though, she realised now, expecting him to wave some magic wand that would have Teddy's problems cleared away. It had been a blow to know Robin was no magician, an even bigger blow to find out he had a hard and selfish streak hidden deep inside of him that had taken a threat to his future with Gerry to bring to the fore. It became all too obvious that he didn't even want to discuss Teddy.

'What about her?' He seemed mystified that she thought Teddy's problems were anything to do with them.

'She's pregnant and has just lost her husband,' she had reminded him, feeling a cold hand of fear clutch at her that Robin wasn't understanding how desperately Teddy needed help. Then the cold fear turned to ice, as Robin said blithely:

'She'll get over it—I don't suppose she's the first girl to be left in that position.'

Gerry came to realising her bath water had grown cold, and sluiced herself off. Funny how she'd seen Robin the other day, she had felt none of the anguish she would have thought she would have done. It had been pure coincidence that she had fainted while he had been there—that and the shock of hearing him telling Crawford the personal details of their relationship. As yet she still didn't know what Robin had been doing in her office—had thought him still in Birmingham. She paused to consider if he had come seeking her out or if he had by some stroke of fate again been transferred and this time to Layton. He'd known she planned to move with Teddy away from the expensive-to-run house in Gringham, but she hadn't thought he'd known where they had moved. Perhaps it was just chance that he happened to call at Arrowsmiths ...

Stepping gingerly out of the bath, Gerry towelled herself dry and sat down on the linen basket feeling ridiculously weak from the effort. With the idea in mind of lying down on her bed for an hour, then getting dressed and going downstairs ready to meet Crawford Arrowsmith if and when he called, she left the bathroom. On the point of crossing the landing, she heard a cry from one of the twins downstairs. She listened and the wail grew louder. Teddy must be at the top end of the garden and out of earshot.

Wrapping her pink dressing gown around her so she wouldn't trip over it, she clutched on to the banister and made her way down to investigate the cry.

Emma was sitting in the middle of the living room carpet when she got there. She had one leg half tucked under her which denoted she had been crawling to enquire into something and had probably come up against something solid. Large glistening tears were rolling down her cheeks as she wailed her anger.

'Oh, you poor baby,' Gerry crooned, bending over her. She heard a movement behind her which denoted that Teddy had come back, then stretched out her arms to pick Emma up, only to find her strength had deserted her. 'Emma baby,' she addressed the child, who had immediately stopped crying when it looked likely she was in for a cuddle. 'You have a poor old thing for an aunt—either that or you've put on two extra stones overnight.'

'I doubt that Emma has put on that much weight during the last few days—more likely you haven't the strength of a gnat,' said a cool voice behind her, and Gerry whirled round—too quickly—to see a business-suited Crawford Arrowsmith giving her a hard look as he studied her face and found the signs of fatigue he was looking for.

Because of her hasty turn round, Gerry momentarily lost her balance, and was forced to cling on to him for a brief moment. When she would have let go his arm, she felt his hand come over the top of hers, forcing her to remain where she was.

How long she stared into those all-seeing, hard grey eyes, she didn't know. She wanted to look away, but felt some magnetism compelling her to hold his look. Then Teddy was coming in from outside, placing some nappies and the peg bag on the kitchen table and coming to scoop Emma up off the floor.

'Hello, Crawford,' she greeted him easily, seeming not to notice Gerry's eyes growing larger in her head, 'I thought I recognised your car outside.'

'How long has Geraldine been up?' he asked, which made Gerry furious enough to give a sharp tug to try and release her hand.

Her hand was held firm. He didn't so much as look at her as he waited for Teddy to answer his question. Anyone would think he suspects I wouldn't give him a truthful answer, Gerry thought, growing angrier by the minute. She had fully intended to be dressed with her hair neatly in a bun, on the offchance that he would call. And now he was here, and her hair was down about her shoulders, the steam from her bath having caused small tendrils of hair to curl about her forehead, and she felt at a decided disadvantage.

Teddy looked from one to the other. 'Gerry was up when I came back from taking the twins out at half past eleven,' she said.

Gerry felt the hand holding hers to his arm tighten its grip as though he was trying to control whatever he felt at Teddy's statement. 'In that case,' he said, 'I think it's about time she was back in bed.' And without wasting time in argument, his arms came around her, and before she knew what was happening, he had picked her up and was making for the stairs.

Gerry was speechless, but not for long. 'Put me down!'

she shrieked, and for the first time in her adult life could cheerfully have slapped Teddy as the smirk on her face grew wider and wider as she watched her outraged sister being carried back to bed in the arms of her employer.

It was a complete waste of breath and energy, Gerry found, trying to get Crawford to listen to her, for his grip on her was firm, telling her he had no intention of putting her down. Once he was in her room, he placed her down on the bed, and she found that she was the one out of breath, whereas his breathing seemed to have altered not at all.

'You're not even out of breath,' she said before she could stop herself.

'Since you weigh less than a skinned rabbit, there's no reason why I should be,' he said smoothly, which further infuriated her, to be likened to a skinned rabbit. 'When did your doctor say you could get out of bed?' Crawford followed on, seeming determined not to acknowledge her anger.

'He didn't.'

'Then I should have thought it was commonsense for you to stay in bed until he instructed you otherwise.' Gerry's lips stayed firmly shut. 'But then you were never long suited in commonsense, were you?' he challenged.

Still she refused to answer him. She had an idea he was as angry as she was, but that he was covering his anger with a cloak of coolness—she knew even if she did let go at him she was bound to come off the loser. It was always the cool one who came off better in an argument.

'So you're going to sulk?'

That got to her as it was meant to, only she didn't realise that until too late. 'I'm not sulking, I'm just—just refusing to argue with you.'

'So you agree with having something to argue about?'

'Yes—yes, I do,' Gerry snapped, then taking a deep breath, plunged on. 'Teddy and I can manage quite well without your—your interference.' It seemed small thanks for the trouble he had been to in getting Mrs Chapman to work for them—but she wasn't having him paying for any help they needed in the cottage. Prepared to go into battle and tell him so, she was shaken to hear the un-checked note of anger in Crawford's voice when he said:

'You little fool—you misguided idiot!' and as her startled eyes flew to his at the vehemence of his tone, 'Why the hell couldn't you tell me what things were like for you at home?—— Or if not tell me, why couldn't you have let the company's welfare department know? Are you so pigheaded, so stubborn, so full of pride that you'd rather kill yourself than let anyone give you a helping hand?'

'Teddy and I were managing all right ...' she started, and got no further.

'The hell you were! I could see you weren't well the first time I set eyes on you—but when I gave you an opening to tell me about your troubles you deliberately let me think Teddy was some man you were living with. You gave no hint that there were any young children, that you were the breadwinner of the family. You deliberately made things worse for yourself by allowing me to draw my own conclusions for your bad time-keeping.'

'Can I help it if you've got a nasty mind?' Gerry came storming back. The firm bed beneath her was giving sup-port to her limbs, and as strength returned to them, so her temper got completely out of hand. 'You were always jib-ing at me,' she went on, her hair bobbing about on her shoulders, her eyes flashing as she tossed her head ready to give him some more. 'You can't blame me if I decided you'd be the last person I would come to if I were in trouble.'

She stopped there as a look passed over his face as though her last statement had staggered him, then the look was gone. 'I'm sorry,' she said quietly, and didn't know why she apologised other than that she felt she was piling ingratitude on top of ingratitude after the way he had gone out of his way to help them. 'I know I sound ungrateful—and you needn't have brought me home. You needn't have got Paul Meadows in to see me, and you needn't have arranged for Mrs Chapman to come in to help.' She felt the threat of tears sting her eyes and blinked rapidly so they wouldn't show. She had no idea why she wanted to cry other than that she never liked losing her temper, and the fact that she was feeling more confused with Crawford Arrowsmith here in her room than at any other time she could remember.

'Some one had to help you, Geraldine,' Crawford said softly, which caused her to want to look at him, only she couldn't if she didn't want him to see how near to tears she was.

Crawford himself seemed to be making a determined effort to damp down his anger, and she couldn't help wondering if it was on account of the fact that he thought she wasn't yet up to receiving the full force of his wrath. She swallowed nervously, grateful for small mercies, as he went on:

'Whether you want to believe it or not, you were heading for a very serious breakdown. Had I known anything of your true circumstances at home I would never have insisted on your spending three nights in London—I imagine you fretted yourself silly wondering how your sister was managing with you away.' Gerry looked hard at the girdle of her dressing gown. She had forgotten Crawford didn't know she had returned home to Little Layton every evening, and felt suddenly guilty at the remorse in his voice. She almost told him the truth then and there, but the moment passed, as he went on, 'This exhaustion you're recovering from has been bad enough, but it could have been far worse—you would have been no help to Teddy or anyone if you'd been allowed to ignore the signs of illness when you fainted last Thursday.'

Gerry looked at him then, and he came to sit beside her on the bed, taking her hand in his. 'You knew I had no intention of going to the medical centre, didn't you? Is that why you insisted on driving me home?'

There was a short silence as she waited for him to answer, then very quietly, he said, 'I'm learning more and more about you, Geraldine, every time I come into contact with you.' Which as an answer, she thought, was somewhat obscure—and she didn't know that she wanted him to know too much about her anyway. She had to have some reserves left if, when she returned to Arrowsmiths, he was still occupying Mr Gillett's office.

Then Crawford stood up from the bed and looked down at her. 'And now I think it's time you were inside those covers—you must be feeling tired, though I know it's the last thing you'll admit.'

Gerry knew he was waiting for her to get into bed, and felt embarrassed colour flood her cheeks as it came to her that he expected her to shed her dressing gown while he was standing there. She hated that she blushed, and hoped he hadn't noticed—though she should have known better. For she felt his eyes on her, and knew he was silently querying the reason for her sudden colour.

'I'll get into bed when you've gone,' she said into her chest, and found he had placed a finger beneath her chin and was tilting her head until she just had to look into his slate grey eyes. She saw they held a teasing light in their depth—it had the effect of sending her embarrassment on its way.

'Anyone would think I'd never seen you in your nightdress before,' he said, and grinned at her in such a way her heart set up a rapid tumbling motion. It wasn't quietened in any way when he leaned forward and placed his warm mouth against her own. Then he stood back from the bed and looked at her, and again she felt an invisible thread keeping her eyes fixed to his. 'I don't suppose for a mo-

ment that will disturb your sleep,' he said, and strangely
Gerry wondered whether she'd heard a note of regret in
his voice before she put it down to the confusion he had
put her into. 'But in case it does, I'm sure Teddy will be
up with your tablets in a few minutes.'

She stared at the door for a long while after he had
gone. What had happened to the short, sharp words she
was going to have with him on the subject of Mrs Chapman? Gerry put Mrs Chapman out of her mind. As soon
as she got back to the office she would settle with Crawford
what he had so far paid Mrs Chapman—for the moment
she was still too awe-stricken to realise how very charming he could be when he put himself to it.

His surmise, though, that Teddy would be up in a few
minutes was very far out. She listened for the sound of his
car departing, and when after twenty minutes had gone
by and still no sound of his car, she began to wonder if
she had missed it—it was a very silent car, after all. Then
she heard the sound of him taking his leave at the door,
and very shortly afterwards heard the purr of his car as it
left the kerb.

When Teddy came in with her tablets shortly afterwards, Gerry thought she looked extremely bright. 'Here
we are, my little chickabiddee,' she said breezily, in a way
Gerry hadn't seen since before she had married Mark, as
she handed her the dosage prescribed by Paul Meadows.

Gerry thought she might tell her something of what
she had been talking about with Crawford as she waited
with her hand outstretched for the glass—but she didn't.
And as she handed the glass back to her, the tablets
swallowed, Gerry looked at her sister and could have sworn
she had an 'I know something you don't know' look on her
face. And for all their closeness, she felt she couldn't ask
her twin the question that it suddenly seemed vital she
knew the answer to—the question of 'What were you and
Crawford talking about?'

Teddy didn't stay long in the room. 'I'll just pop in and take a look at the twins, then I must go and put the place tidy in case Paul Meadows takes it into his head to put you first on his list tomorrow morning.'

It was the first indication Gerry had had that Paul Meadows would be calling to see her the next day, but that didn't perturb her too much—it was natural, she supposed, that he would keep an eye on her. No, the thing that fretted away at her just before the tablets she had swallowed began their work and sent her off into a relaxing sleep that unwound her nerve ends was why should it bother her what Crawford and her sister had been talking about? Teddy had laughed at the idea that Crawford might be interested in her, and anyway, even if he was interested in Teddy, she was sure she wasn't in the least put out. She didn't like that satisfied look on Teddy's face, though ...

CHAPTER SEVEN

PAUL MEADOWS called the next morning, and he, like Crawford the night before, spent some time in talking to Teddy before he came up to see his patient. Gerry felt a quiver of alarm shoot through her that grew with every minute of the fifteen it took him to come and see her. Were the twins ill? Was Teddy keeping back from her that something had happened to one, or both, of them?

'Are the twins all right?' was her first question as he came through the door with Teddy close behind him.

'What a little worry madam you are!' His smile relieved the tension of her mind. She liked the way Paul Meadows' eyes smiled when he smiled—she'd noticed that sometimes Crawford could give the impression of being in a good humour when his eyes were positively chilly. 'I've never seen such a pair of perfect specimens as Emma and Sarah,' he went on to clear any remaining doubts. 'Now let's take a look at you and see how near to being perfect you are.'

His examination didn't take long, as he addressed questions to both her and Teddy. 'I think we can cut the tablets down to one after each meal now,' he said, addressing Teddy, then closing his case, turned to Gerry and told her she could get up for the afternoon. Gerry's eyes flew to Teddy hoping she wasn't going to give away she had been out of bed yesterday, then looking back to Paul Meadows she saw a look on his face that told her he had guessed anyway. 'Just remember to take things quietly,' he told her, adding, 'Teddy has proved her worth as a nurse—it would be unfair of you to undo all the effort she's put in in looking after you.'

Gerry thought over his words when he had gone. Teddy had obviously gone up by leaps and bounds in his estimation—he'd even called her Teddy when he'd been referring to her, she remembered. But he was right about one thing, she thought, and even though she knew it would irritate her not to be up and doing once she was downstairs, she agreed that it wouldn't be fair to Teddy if in so doing she undid all her sister's efforts while she had been ill.

'He's clever, isn't he?' said Teddy, coming back into the room after seeing him out. 'I'm certain he knows you got up yesterday.' A sudden thought struck her. 'I say, you don't suppose Crawford has been in touch with him and told him, do you?'

Gerry's eyes grew wide at the thought. She wouldn't put it past him, she was beginning to think, before commonsense—the commonsense Crawford thought she was short suited on—reared its head. 'I shouldn't think so for a minute,' she rejected the idea. 'Why should he bother? I'm only a P.A. he happens to employ, after all. He only comes here anyway because I happened to pass out in front of him—I expect he sees it as a sort of duty to check up that I'm on the mend. Besides, the sooner I am better the sooner I'll be back at work—and that's what concerns him most.'

She wasn't sure why she was saying all this. Teddy didn't seem particularly interested anyway, and had her back to her as she stood gazing out of the window. I know he's not interested in me for any reason other than that I'm an employee, Gerry thought, and felt an odd sort of let-down feeling inside her that had her turning her mind completely away from thoughts of Crawford Arrowsmith.

'How long has Paul Meadows been calling you Teddy?' she asked, and Teddy turned back from the window to come to stand at the foot of the bed.

'That was the first time—and it wasn't directly to me then, was it?' Teddy commented with a thoughtful look growing on her face. 'I thought he couldn't stand me. Did you hear what he said about my proving my worth as a nurse, though?' Teddy looked flattered for a moment, as though she still couldn't believe she had heard him correctly. Then one of the twins started crying and the other one joined in in sympathy. 'Peace is over,' Teddy had her hand on the bedroom door. 'I'd better go and see to them before they start bashing each other!'

Mindful of what Paul Meadows had said about not undoing Teddy's good work, Gerry tried her hardest over the next week to heed his advice. It helped, she had to admit, having Mrs Chapman about the place—though she was still worried about how they were going to manage to pay her. For the moment Crawford was attending to her wages, but Gerry had every intention of reimbursing him the next time she saw him.

She had seen nothing of him since that day he had carried her back to bed, and in the week that followed and he hadn't come, she had ceased listening for every car that purred past their door. Countless times to begin with she had thought each one would stop and it would be him, but it was only a car changing gear ready for the climb where the end of their road began an incline up a hill. The flutterings she had experienced inside at the thought that each car might be him she could not so easily put to one side. But she managed in the end to convince herself it was pure nervousness, because now that she was so much better —she hoped Paul Meadows would say she could return to work soon—she knew she would be tackling the subject of Mrs Chapman with Crawford, and had an instinctive feeling it wasn't going to be easy.

It was two weeks before she saw him again, and by that time she had put on weight, fully recovered her strength, and had made up her mind that very morning to go down to Paul Meadows' surgery that night and tell him she would be returning to work next Monday. As her own health improved, there had been a dramatic change in Teddy too. It warmed Gerry's heart to see that her sister no longer cried as easily as she had been prone to do. In fact, she suddenly thought, she couldn't remember Teddy giving way to the sadness of her thoughts once in the last two weeks. She could see her now from the kitchen window— Teddy was playing with the twins on the lawn while she prepared a salad for lunch. Absently Gerry noted that she would have to get the ancient mower out soon or the grass would be too long to tackle by machine—Teddy had a glow about her these days, and she couldn't help wondering if it could *all* be put down to their having Mrs Chapman to help out.

Because it was such a sunny day and sacrilege to be indoors, they had their meal outside on the lawn, and after they had settled the twins in the shade to have their nap, both girls stretched out in shorts and tops and felt at peace with the world. It was some time later when Teddy broke the silence.

'Thirsty?' she asked into the quiet of the afternoon.

'Could drink gallons,' Gerry murmured, near to dozing off.

'Go and get some squash,' Teddy coaxed, near to dozing off herself.

'All right.' Gerry made to get to her feet.

'No, you stay—I'll go. Just remembered my new leaf!'

'You've turned one over, you mean?' Gerry was coming wide awake.

'Well, not before time, was it? I was a bit of a lazy slob.'

'Oh, Teddy, no—you weren't,' Gerry protested. 'You had ...'

'No excuses,' Teddy refused to allow Gerry to defend her. 'I'll go and get that squash—with ice!'

Gerry smiled softly as Teddy disappeared into the cottage, then lay down and closed her eyes again. She had never thought of Teddy as a lazy slob—Teddy had had a terrible time, losing both her adored father and Mark at the same time.

Something tickled her bare foot, and she wiggled her toes to flick it off. But it came again, so she moved her foot about six inches. Then as her foot still tickled, and still with her eyes closed, she drew her foot towards her intending to brush the offending insect away with her hand —but her hand came into contact with another hand, warm and masculine. Instantly her eyes came open, and she stared in eye-blinking amazement. She was holding hands with Crawford Arrowsmith.

Wordlessly, her eyes caught and held by those grey eyes, she stared at him. She saw a smile break from his lips, and for one of the few times since she had known him, she saw the smile light up in his eyes.

'You looked so peaceful lying there,' he said, his deep-noted voice sounding neither cool nor remote as she was used to, but easy somehow. 'It seemed a shame to disturb you—but I couldn't resist it.' He let go her hand and came and sat down on the grass beside her, making her overwhelmingly conscious of the shortness of her shorts showing off the full length of her long slender legs, and the clinging vest top that showed up the curves beneath.

'Teddy's in the house,' she blurted out, needing to say something, but her mind refusing to come up with anything very brilliant. It confused her to have Crawford's eyes running over her dressed as she was, when always before she had tried to give the impression of a cool, efficient P.A. in her body-concealing, badly fitting—she now owned—outer garments. She refused at that point to remember that Crawford had seen her in her nightie.

Crawford finished his inspection of her. 'I came to see you.' He was still easy with her, but she felt she couldn't relax her guard.

'I'm coming back to work on Monday.' She wished her voice didn't sound so staccato, but he was having that effect on her. She wondered if Teddy would see him from the kitchen window—where had she got to anyway? If she was deliberately keeping out of the way she couldn't be making a better job of it. Perhaps she'd see him and think to bring her wrap-around skirt when she brought the squash out.

'Who says you're coming back to work on Monday?' Crawford's voice was conversational, so she thought he had accepted without argument that she was well enough to return to the office.

'I'm quite fit now,' she said. 'I shall go and see Paul Meadows tonight—but,' she added hurriedly, for she thought she detected the smile had gone out of Crawford's eyes, 'only as a courtesy.' It was only polite, she reasoned, to let Paul Meadows give her the formal 'O.K.' to return to work.

'I'll give him a ring myself,' Crawford said, and it sounded so natural the way he said it—as if he had every right to ring her physician and enquire about her health.

'There's no need for you ...' she began hotly, when Crawford lay back on the grass and closed his eyes; now she could read nothing from his expression. She looked at him as he lay there, casually dressed in fine slacks and short-sleeved sports shirt, his arms showing off a wealth of short dark hairs. She dragged her eyes away from him and forced herself to think clearly. 'You've phoned him before, haven't you?' she accused, but tempering her accusation with a deceptively mild tone. She was convinced suddenly that he had telephoned Paul Meadows that day she had been out of bed without Paul's say-so.

Crawford sat up, looked at her for a long moment, seemed to read the mutiny in her expression, then stood up. 'Come for a drive.'

It was just as though he hadn't heard a word she said, she thought, as he calmly ignored her accusation. 'It's too hot.' She had no intention of driving with him ever.

'It won't be.'

He made it sound a pure statement of fact. How did one begin to argue against his all male self-confidence? Then she had no time to answer anything, for he was stretching down a hand to her, and whether she wanted to stand up or not, she was being pulled up until she was standing close to him.

'I don't suppose you've been out anywhere since you've been ill?' he questioned.

She thought better than to tell him she'd never gone out before she'd been ill—she didn't want him to interfere any further in her life. 'I've been down to the village shops a couple of times.'

He didn't say he'd bet that was one big thrill, he had no need to—his look said it for him. 'Stop acting like some temperamental female and come with me,' he said.

'A breath of fresh air will work wonders for your complexion.'

'Thanks!'

He grinned at her sarcastic thanks at his remark which she took to mean her complexion could do with freshening up. She liked his grin, loath though she was to admit it—liked it so much she found herself grinning idiotically back; she didn't want to do that either.

Crawford took hold of her hand, urging her to go with him down the garden path. 'You know you have a beautiful complexion anyway,' he said, when she had straightened the grin from her face. It pleased her that he thought so, but before she could question why then did she need a breath of air, they were at the bottom of the path. From being certain she wasn't driving anywhere with him, she was now undecided what to do. 'Now what?' he asked, when she dug her heels in and refused to move another step.

'If I'm going driving—I'm going to change.' It seemed her mind had decided for her—she had no say in the matter of whether she wanted to go with him or not.

Her words had his eyes going over her again, and she wished she hadn't said anything as his eyes rested briefly on her breasts. She knew he was aware she hadn't a bra on, and colour flooded her face. As he witnessed the pink in her cheeks, a gentle smile lit Crawford's eyes, and far from the acid comment Gerry expected him to make at her prevarications, he said, 'I'll give you five minutes.'

She met Teddy coming out of the living room. 'Where did you get to?' she asked before realising her question was unnecessary, for Teddy was decently covered in a cotton frock. 'Crawford's here.' Again unnecessary, for Teddy like herself had been happily oblivious of how they might appear to male eyes in their scanty attire. 'He's taking me driving—he's given me five minutes to change.'

'You've just used up one of them,' Teddy said laughingly.

Gerry raced upstairs, donned fresh underwear and pulled out a pretty cotton dress that was three years old. Dragging the dress over her head, she realised she had one minute to spare, before she stopped to wonder, why on earth was she racing around like someone on fire? She hadn't asked Crawford to call—and while he might be her boss, she was still on sick leave. And if he took it into his head to do the dutiful employer bit and take her out for a drive, then he could wait until she was ready.

Seating herself in front of the dressing table mirror, she ran a comb through her hair. She then dragged her hair back from her face—she didn't like it that way, never had liked that screwed-up bun, but it had seemed necessary at the time. She let go her hair, leaving it to hang loosely on her shoulders. Crawford had seen her with her hair down now—she wasn't going to win any points for antagonising him; he didn't like her hair screwed back either, she recalled, remembering the day he had brought her home. She had told him she had a headache and he had taken the pins out of her hair. It had seemed so natural then, but now it seemed an intimate gesture and she could no longer bear looking back at her reflection in the mirror. Her eyes were seeming to be telling her something she didn't want to admit to—though she had to admit to the growing feeling of excitement that was suddenly surging through her veins.

When Gerry saw the Aston Martin Volante convertible parked outside Honeysuckle Cottage, she understood what Crawford had meant when he'd said it wouldn't be too hot to go for a drive. He made sure she was comfortable, then got into the vehicle beside her. She waited for him to switch on the ignition, and when he didn't do so, she looked across at him to see him pulling something from his trousers pocket.

'That's my scarf,' she said, her eyes growing wide as if expecting him to take out a pair of performing doves next.

'True,' Crawford agreed. 'Knowing the vanity of women, I asked Teddy for something to keep your hair from blowing about—put it on.'

Not meaning to be contrary but her pride pricked at his reference to the vanity of women, instead of putting the scarf on peasant fashion as she was sure he was expecting, Gerry elected to make a bandeau from it and tied it underneath the back of her hair—it would keep her hair out of her eyes anyway. Crawford gave her a smooth look which told her she'd done exactly what he'd expected her to do.

Determined to ignore him and enjoy the drive, Gerry did just that, and felt the exhilaration of the wind feathering past her face, the cooling breeze giving fresh life to her limbs in what had turned out to be a scorching day. Crawford drove fast and drove well, slowing down when the road conditions required it, and stopping altogether when they reached one or two beauty spots.

'Everybody seems to have the same idea today,' he remarked when they came to one plateau that looked over several counties where a few other cars were parked. They got out of the car to have a look at the view. 'Want an ice-cream?' Without waiting for her answer, which she had to own would have been yes, Crawford went to wait in the small queue that had formed by the vehicle of an enterprising ice-cream salesman who had chosen to try his luck there.

When Crawford returned, she saw he had bought two cornets, a single one for himself and a double one for her. Everybody's trying to fatten me up, she couldn't help thinking—her eyes saying as much. She knew Crawford had read her thoughts, and blurted out, 'I've put on four pounds.'

'It suits you,' was all he said, and he turned to look at the patchwork vista before them.

Gerry saw massive acreages were broken into roughly squared off fields by hedges of brambles and trees. Far into the distance were clutches of buildings that spoke of small villages, all going peacefully about their business in the still of the afternoon. It was beautiful up there on the plateau and Gerry stared at the view entranced, mindless of the cornet she was clutching until the ice-cream began to melt and she had to hastily lick her fingers.

Giving her ice-cream more attention now, she nibbled at the rest of it until it had all gone, and turned to Crawford to find him watching her. 'Stick out your tongue,' he instructed, giving her no clue as to why she should do such a thing.

A devilish gleam appeared in her eyes at the opportunity. She just couldn't resist the temptation, for all she had no idea of his sudden command. Not only did she stick out her tongue, she wrinkled her nose as well. Then she saw Crawford's hand come up and felt him moisten his handkerchief from her tongue and instantly closed her mouth, to find him wiping away a smear of ice-cream from the corner of her mouth.

'You're getting cheeky,' he said, 'a sure sign you're getting better.' His voice was light and she was smiling at him when he explained, 'I merely thought you would prefer your own spit to mine.'

Back in the car, Crawford turned off the main road and drove slowly this time, through leafy lanes in the peaceful countryside. And it was a time of enchantment to Gerry just to sit back feeling the breeze ruffling her hair, and watch the trees and hedgerows sail by. Then they turned off the main road on to another road and then on to another that was no more than a track where Crawford found a shady part and turned off the engine. She gave him an anxious glance that wasn't lost on him. It seemed to her that this out-of-the-way spot couldn't be known to very many people, and she suspicioned he had the idea of bringing her to this isolated location from the very beginning.

'Take that alarmed look off your face, Geraldine,' she was bidden, 'the driver has relaxation in mind—not seduction.'

'I never thought you had,' she replied quickly.

'No?'

'No.'

'Then you haven't been around as much as a girl of your age usually has.'

'I'm only twenty-four, for goodness' sake!' The way he was going on you'd think I was ninety, she thought, getting rattled when she didn't want to. This was such a lovely spot.

'Exactly,' said Crawford, and she didn't understand what 'Exactly' meant until he continued, 'Not many twenty-four-year-olds are still starry-eyed virgins.'

'You'd know, of course,' she came back hotly, her colour rising.

He ignored that, and turned in his seat to give her the full benefit of his slate grey eyes that seemed to have darkened. 'Didn't Robin Preston ever try to seduce you— he was hoping to marry you?'

If he could ignore her comments, she could ignore his, though she was beginning to feel that fluttering sensation again. Needing some small action, she raised her hand and removed the bandeau from her hair. 'Where did Robin go, by the way?' she asked, thinking to turn the conversation. 'He was in the room when I passed out—when I came to he'd disappeared.'

'I sent him about his business—went back to his own office, I shouldn't wonder.' Crawford sounded completely unconcerned with what had happened to Robin. Gerry could just see Crawford, taking in his stride that she'd dropped in a heap at his feet, picking her up without turning a hair and calmly ordering Robin out. Then the implication of what Crawford had just said came hurrying in.

'You sent Robin back to his own office, you said—you mean Robin works at Arrowsmith Electronics?'

'Didn't you know?—Perhaps you didn't.' Crawford looked thoughtful as he answered his own question. 'I believe he started with the company on the Monday you were working in London,' he paused. 'The day he came looking for you would have been the first chance he would have of seeing you.' She had to admire Crawford for his deduction, but he was out with his guesswork with his next remark. 'Is that the first time you've seen him since you broke your engagement?'

'We weren't engaged.'

'Yet he thought he was going to marry you?'

'I thought so too,' said Gerry without realising she had spoken. Then could have bitten her tongue out, because Crawford already knew too much about her personal life without her volunteering any more.

'What happened?'

He was too inquisitive by far. Why should he be interested in what happened? It didn't matter to him at all, and she was damned if she'd satisfy his curiosity. Crawford's look was piercing through her, so she deliberately turned her head away. Let him gather from that that she had no intention of answering any more of his questions. She was unprepared for the hand that came beneath her chin and forced her head round until she was looking at him.

'You said in the office that day that it was over twelve months since you'd seen him, and I received a very clear impression that day that he didn't think very much of Teddy.' There was a pause while Crawford got all his conclusions neatly in order, then, 'From what your sister has told me, it was around that time her husband died. Would I be right in thinking you gave Preston up in order to look after her?'

Gerry refused to answer him. She couldn't turn her head

away, but she didn't have to look at him either. She looked
down at the masculine column of his throat, saw the darker
hair growing up from his chest through the opening in
his sports shirt, and feeling decidedly agitated, closed her
eyes.

'That's just the sort of misguided thing I'm growing to
think you would do,' he told her harshly when she refused
to open her eyes. 'It's typical of you, isn't it? To throw
away the chance of making a happy married life for yourself because your sister's marriage ended tragically—it
wouldn't occur to you to take your problem to someone
else, would it? No, you have to take it all on yourself—
you'd have killed yourself doing it too if I hadn't decided I was going to see what this Teddy thought he was
playing at letting you go around looking half dead.'

Abruptly Gerry opened her eyes, wrenching her chin
from his grasp as angry sparks of fire leapt from her eyes,
and for one of the rare times in her life, incensed by the
hard way he was slating her, she lost her temper.

'What the hell do you know about anything?' she
stormed. 'Teddy's husband wasn't the only one to die in
the car crash that killed him—my father died too. The
house we lived in was rented at a sky-high rent—Teddy
was left penniless—she would never have been able to
afford to take on the tenancy. I would have been all right,
wouldn't I, starting out with everything rosy in my life—
my marriage, with a destitute sister awaiting the arrival of
her babies. Tell me what you would have done, Mr Arrowsmith. Go on, you just tell me what you would have done?'

Still angry, though her temper was spent, Gerry looked
at him furiously. She was aware she was shaking uncon-
trollably, and as her anger began to simmer down, she
knew she was near to tears.

For answer, Crawford leaned over and hauled her up
against him, not saying a word until her trembling had

lessened. Gerry wanted to pull indignantly away from him, but she felt too spent to move. Then very quietly, Crawford began to ask her questions, none of the harshness in his voice she had heard earlier. She hadn't intended telling him another thing, but his very gentleness with her, so much a contrast from the way he had been, had her revealing that she and Teddy had moved from Gringham, a town which lay fifteen miles the other side of Layton from where they now lived. He was finding out how the landlord had someone else wanting to rent the house in Gringham and had offered them the cottage they now lived in. She didn't tell him that even with the smaller accommodation, the rent was still quite high—but it had come more into line with her pocket when she'd been lucky enough to get the job at Arrowsmiths.

And then Crawford was apologising for goading her into losing her temper, while managing to sound as though he wasn't sorry at all at having extracted from her in her anger what he had wanted to know. She had an odd sort of feeling he had deliberately goaded her into losing her temper so she would reveal things that normally galloping horses wouldn't have dragged from her to an outsider. Yet was he such an outsider? From what he had said, it seemed he had made up his mind to have a look at her home conditions before he ever knew Teddy was not the male he had expected to see.

'You think I'm pretty much of a monster, don't you?' Crawford questioned from above her head. His voice was gentle, and she knew she should pull away from him, but it was so comforting having his arms around her, her body wouldn't obey what her mind was telling her.

'I wouldn't go as far as to say that,' she replied, thinking perhaps she had over-dramatised what she had told him—for all it had been fact—and trying to inject humour into what for her had been an intense few moments. 'Brute and bully perhaps—but monster, well ...' Her voice trailed off and she felt his chest move beneath her cheek in silent laughter.

Feeling calmer, her remark having lightened the tension between them, Gerry made to move away from him. But his hand on the side of her face held her against him, and as his hand began an absentminded caressing of her chin, and followed through up to her ear, she knew she would have to move away from him soon because there was a riotous jangling up her nerve ends that she had never experienced from a man's touch before, not even with Robin. Pushing her left hand against his chest, she levered herself away, and felt a vague sense of disappointment at how easily Crawford let her go.

'I said you have beautiful bone structure,' he told her, his eyes lingering over her face. 'I'll bet you photograph superbly.'

Gerry had to give a nervous cough before she answered, and wished she hadn't because now he was aware she was just that teeny bit unsure of herself with him. 'What a pity you haven't got your camera,' she said airily, and watched as he grinned.

'It would take a more professional cameraman than I to do you justice,' he said, and the word justice made her remember she hadn't yet taxed him with the unfairness of allowing him to pay for Mrs Chapman's services.

'Oh, by the way,' she said, trying to make her voice sound casual, as if she had never fretted and worried for a moment on the subject. 'I—er——' she lost the casual note as she sought for a tactful way to tell him kind though his gesture had been, the responsibility was hers. 'Thank you very much for arranging about Mrs Chapman,' she tried again, and was thankful she could bring the good lady's name out without faltering. 'It was very good of you, and Teddy and I both appreciate what you did—but

I'll pay Mrs Chapman from now on. I've calculated how much you've paid her to date ...' She didn't like at all the ominous silence that was coming from Crawford, but having got this far she wanted it over and done with. She reached her hand down the side of her in search of her handbag, and felt rather than saw Crawford's hand snake across and grip her wrist in such a blood-stemming hold, she thought her wrist would break.

Her eyes flew to his, and a gasp of alarm escaped her at the fury in his face. 'For once in your damned life let somebody do something to help you!' She flinched from the anger in him, and only sheer outrage as the thought came to her that it was only from pity that he wanted to help had her finding her voice.

'We're not charity cases yet, you know.'

At her words, the grip on her wrist tightened and she was sure he was going to break it in two. But she didn't know suddenly which was the worst pain, the grip he had on her wrist or the bewildering tightness within her—the uncertain yet certain feeling that she was on the brink of some shattering discovery. Some of the pain she was feeling must have been showing in her eyes, for Crawford scanned her face as if seeking for the cause of her anxious look. Then he seemed to become aware of his bruising hold on her, and looked down at the wrist in his grip and slowly let her go, staring hard at the reddened flesh his hand had left behind.

'You stretch my patience to the limit, Geraldine,' he said tightly, which she thought was as much of an apology as she was likely to get as he recovered his control.

Why she felt the need to explain why she couldn't accept his help, she couldn't have said, but she felt torn two ways. She wanted to tell him she appreciated the thought behind his deed—Teddy had obviously needed some help since she herself was out of action; Teddy just wouldn't have been able to cope with looking after her and the twins, and be able to fit the housework in as well. But he must see they had to be independent.

'I don't mean to appear ungrateful,' she began, feeling unhappy that that was exactly what he was thinking—he'd already done far more than most employers in his position would think of doing. 'It's just that Teddy and I have to manage on our own.'

'But you can't manage on your own, can you?'

She didn't like the blunt way he was speaking. It told her he was still as mad as hell with her. 'We can—now that I'm better,' she came back, refusing to admit defeat.

'And how long will it be before you knock yourself up again?' He didn't wait for her to answer, but went on, 'As I saw it, it was either get someone in like Mrs Chapman to relieve your sister so she could look after you, or get you admitted into hospital. Since your sister very nearly had hysterics at the idea of you going into hospital—though for the life of me I can't think why ...'

'Teddy can't be left on her own at night,' Gerry butted in, quick to defend her sister. 'She has a thing about it ...' Her voice tailed off as Crawford looked at her, a frightening still expression on his face that she couldn't find a reason for until she realised what she had just said.

'What exactly, would you mind telling me,' he asked, enunciating every word clearly, 'did dear Teddy do while you were staying with your aunt in London?'

She knew she had started to tremble again. The look on his face was fearsome, as if he was anticipating her answer. They were all alone in this secluded country lane, not a soul had passed, and she was beginning to think from the expression on his face that he was ready to commit near murder if she confirmed the suspicion that was growing in his mind. But, as thought chased after thought in her mind, she could come up with nothing but the truth if he was insistent on getting an answer—and she was sure Crawford Arrowsmith was a man who would insist on just that.

CHAPTER EIGHT

'I'M waiting, Geraldine.' Not with a lot of patience either, Gerry thought. 'Tell me now what your sister did for a night attendant while you were staying with your aunt in London.'

She was glad he was being sarcastic, it took some of the sting out of his murderous look. 'I don't have an aunt in London,' she confessed quietly.

'Then might I ask with whom you stayed the three nights you were there?'

'I didn't stay in London.'

There, it was out. She put her hands defensively behind her back in case he took it into his head to grab hold of her wrist again in that punishing hold.

'You didn't stay in London?' he repeated incredulously, as if scarcely believing the words that had just sounded in his ears. 'You're not telling me you journeyed there and back morning and evening?'

She didn't know what he was making such a fuss about. 'You do it,' she accused, not knowing for sure, but feeling he might have done sometimes.

'That's beside the point,' he snapped. 'I have a fast car in perfect condition—— My God,' he exclaimed, as though the thought had just struck him, 'you didn't travel by train—you journeyed all that way in that deathtrap of a car!'

'Deathtrap?' she repeated, her eyes involuntarily going to his and glad to see that although he was still looking as though he couldn't believe any of what she was telling him, now that the worst was over, some of what she'd said having sunk in, he didn't look nearly so murderous as he had done.

'I said deathtrap, and that's exactly what it is,' he said testily, letting her know her question was getting in the way of the issue they were discussing. 'I've had your car—for the want of a better word—examined by the transport department. I found the engineer's report on my desk when I returned from the States yesterday.' She hadn't known he had been abroad. 'From all the faults and failings the engineer found, it made me shudder to think that anyone would be idiotic enough to take it out of a garage, let alone drive it—— And to think you travelled the distance of Little Layton to London and back in it, not once, but three times!'

Gerry took her eyes off him. If her car was as bad as he said it was—and she couldn't doubt his word—she shuddered herself to think what would have happened to Teddy if she'd been injured or maimed and unable to work to keep them. Then a more sobering thought hit her. If the poor old A35 was in such a bad condition as Crawford was telling her, what hope had she got of its passing its M.O.T. test next month? She could never hope to afford to pay for repairs. Sheer hopelessness struck her at that point, and tears of misery sprang to her eyes. She looked down at her lap so that Crawford wouldn't witness them. How was she going to get to work? The bus service was less than useless—and how about those weekend trips? They never journeyed very far, admitted, but it gave Teddy a break and she looked forward to their little jaunts.

'And what time did you have to get up in the morning in order to be in the London office on time?' Crawford wasn't yet ready to let her off the hook, then. She had nothing further to lose by telling him, she thought, her despair about the car outweighing everything else.

'Five o'clock,' she said in a choked sort of voice, and with a feeling of tell the truth and get it all over with, 'and in answer to your next question—it was anything between eight and nine before I got home in the evening.' Then to her horror, she burst into tears, and didn't know who was the most surprised—her or Crawford.

'Gerry!' he exclaimed, aghast, using the shortened version of her name for the first time. And for the second time that afternoon she felt herself being hauled up against him as his arms came around her. 'I didn't mean to make you cry,' he was saying in a low voice, and she couldn't tell him it wasn't his fault she was crying. He couldn't know how much it meant to her to have the A35 in a roadworthy condition. She needed all her strength to try and stem the flow of tears.

Then Crawford was talking quietly to her, stroking her hair, agreeing with her earlier opinion that he was a brute and a bully—the shock of which successfully stopped her sobbing, but she could do nothing to stop the tears from welling up in her eyes and rolling down her cheeks. 'You're such a fighter— it never entered my head you'd give way to tears,' he was saying quietly. 'You wouldn't be crying now, I know, only you haven't been well.' His voice hardened slightly. 'If only you'd given me a hint of your circumstances I would never have insisted on your going to London. As it is, you were up at the crack of dawn, working a full day and then driving home again, all the time getting more and more exhausted—it's no wonder you fainted!'

Realising Crawford was loathing all of his part in all this, even though he hadn't known at the time the strain he had placed on her, Gerry raised her head to tell him it was in no way his fault. But as she did so, she found his head was bent down towards her, and was much much closer than she had imagined. He didn't pull his head back as she would have supposed he would do, and, her eyes fastened on his, she found herself unable to pull back either. When his head came nearer and he paused giving her the chance to retreat, there was no thought in her mind to do so. And when his lips covered hers, it was all she needed at that moment to salve the unhappiness within her.

Crawford's kiss was gentle across her mouth at first. But when his arms tightened about her, some instinct all its own had her arms going up about him, and as his kiss deepened, his mouth searching her lips with his, she pressed to get closer to him, and let herself go to the joy of the moment. Her lips parted at his experienced probing, and she felt the springy softness of his hair as her fingers moved from his neck upwards.

Then Crawford too seemed to want to get closer, and her breasts crushed against his solid chest, she clung to him while he traced kisses down the side of her face to her ear, before claiming her lips once more, until her senses were heightened to a pitch of barely conscious thought.

Crawford released his tight hold on her slightly in order to let one hand make caressing movements down her spine, his hand sensitively trailing over her hip and upwards to her waist. She was mindless to the fact he had unbuttoned her dress from waist to neckline, as again she felt both his arms come to encircle her. And again they were locked together and she could feel the warmth of his body against hers, and her own mouth left his to place fluttering kisses to the side of his face. Then once more he was holding her with only one arm, and as their lips met again, her lips parting invitingly, she felt the warm caress of his hand sliding her dress from off her shoulders, her bra being no hindrance as with a practised touch its straps were slipped away. And in as many seconds as it took for her to realise what was happening, his hand was cupping her breast, and as with shock sanity tried to make itself comprehended, Crawford's lips left her mouth and were transferred to the rosy sweet crown of her breast.

Her gasp was audible at where their passion was leading—her voice husky and unlike her own, and almost a whimper as she begged, 'No—— Oh, Crawford—no!'

Crawford's lips left her breast as her words reached him, only for their place to be taken over by his warm palm as his thumb caressed its throbbing tip. 'I won't hurt you,' he said huskily, and Gerry thought she would die with the pain of having to refuse him as something deep within her was telling her she must. When his lips would have claimed hers yet again, it took all her will power to turn her head away.

'No, Crawford,' she said again, and as his body stilled, his hand over her breast stayed its mind-bending touch, she managed in a voice that was only slightly stronger, 'I don't want to.'

Crawford's hand dropped away from her breast. The arm that had been around her was withdrawn, and both hands descended on her waist in a crushingly tight hold as he fought for the control to accept that she meant what she said.

'You could damn well have fooled me,' he said harshly, and while his words were still grating in her ears, he was outside the car and had gone to stand some yards away with his back towards her.

Gerry tried not to cry as she pushed her bra straps back on to her shoulders. She had nothing to cry about, she thought, as she rebuttoned her dress which mysteriously she had never felt coming apart. Crawford had accepted that she didn't want to go along the path it had seemed more than likely he was taking her down—so what had she got to cry about? Nothing, nothing at all, she thought, as she replaced the bandeau round her head and tears rained from her eyes. Nothing to cry about except that Crawford was now hating the very sight of her—and she, God help her, had just realised he meant more to her than even Teddy. While he was standing over there, his back rigid, hating her like hell, she had just discovered something that had been staring her in the face for ages, only she had been too blind to see it. She was hopelessly in love with him.

So lost was she in the agony of her feelings, she didn't hear him come back. And it wasn't until he was sitting beside her pushing a crisp white handkerchief into her hands that she came to. When the handkerchief came across and she was instructed tersely, 'Mop your face,' she gave an involuntary start of surprise, and was told bluntly, 'Hang on to your maidenly virtue—I'm not likely to try anything like that again.'

'I thought when we stopped here you said you didn't have seduction in mind,' she retorted, which was a good effort, she thought, seeing how nothing seemed to be making sense any more.

'I didn't—take my word for it,' he came back coldly. 'I just never expected to have so much—co-operation.'

That hurt. It hurt badly, and Gerry wasn't sure at that moment which was the worst wounded, her pride or the fact that he seemed to have the impression she went around kissing everyone like that. 'That's the first time I've ...' her voice became strangled at that point, and Crawford finished for her.

'It's the first time you've been that far—— Do you think I'm unaware of that fact?' His voice was cutting into her painfully. 'The next time you take it into your head to try a little experimenting—be careful who you pick on. He might not be as ... accommodating as I am.'

She wanted to tell him there would never be another time, but had the sense to realise he might begin to wonder why. The new love she had for him was already bruised, she wasn't about to let herself in for further hammering.

'I'm just not in your league, am I?' she said instead.

'Shut up,' he answered, and Gerry knew she would be better off doing just that.

The journey back to Little Layton was made in almost complete silence, Crawford not offering one word to her, which told her how fed up with her company he was. Well, she hadn't asked him to take her on this drive in the first place, she reasoned, glad to feel her fierce pride at work again.

A few miles before Little Layton, she asked him coldly if he would mind pulling in at the next layby for a few moments. She didn't think he had heard her, but when a layby came into view, he reduced the speed of the convertible and drove into it. Without looking at him Gerry took her mirror from her bag. Her eyes were still a shade pink from her weeping.

'If you don't want Teddy to know the truth,' Crawford said coolly, letting her know he didn't give a hoot what she told her sister, 'you could tell her the wind caught your eyes as we went along.'

He didn't have to give her the excuse, though she supposed she was grateful for it. She would never have thought of that herself, and though she didn't want to tell Teddy a lie, this new-found love she had for this cold stranger by her side had to be her secret and no one else's. She closed her bag with a snap, indicating she was now ready to go on. But when Crawford didn't move off but propped his elbow on the windowsill and just looked at her, she was forced to turn to look at him.

'Do I take it your backing down at the last moment this afternoon means you're still in love with Preston?' His voice said he didn't care one way or the other.

'Whether I'm still in love with Robin or not is none of your business,' she said shortly, wanting to cry again that it mattered so little to him that she might be in love with someone else.

A steely look entered Crawford's eyes, and she thought he was going to set about verbally extinguishing her. His lips tightened at the aloofness of her remark, but he had full control of himself as he turned the key in the ignition, and the only thing he said was, 'If you don't want your sister to suspect you're going home——' he paused as though searching for the correct word, then brought out, 'wiser than you left, might I suggest you do your buttons up in the proper buttonholes?'

He put the car into gear and they were moving by the time Gerry's startled eyes looked down, and she saw the front of her bodice was buttoned up anyhow. She had been too shaken to know much of what she'd been doing after Crawford had left the car. The buttons were in the right order when he dropped her at her gate without another word being spoken between them.

She didn't look back to see him drive off—would barely have had time to anyway, she thought. Crawford was off before she had clicked the gate shut, which endorsed the feeling she had that he was utterly fed up with her. Gerry went down the path knowing she had to keep Teddy from guessing anything was wrong. As dear as Teddy was, she didn't think she was up to her questions. She doubted she ever would be—she couldn't find any answers for herself, let alone supply her sister with any.

When she reached the back door, however, she found there was no need to tell Teddy anything. For Teddy was at the top end of the garden, the twins playing happily at her feet, and the man who appeared to be tinkering with the lawnmower was Paul Meadows.

Teddy waved, 'Have a nice drive?' She seemed to be too interested in what Paul Meadows was doing to want to come any nearer.

'Lovely,' Gerry returned. She waved a hand in the general direction of her hair. 'I'll go and tidy up.' Teddy's attention was already back on the lawnmower when she went through the back door and up to her room.

She spared a thought to wonder, without surprise, if it was the lawnmower Teddy was interested in or the doctor, now turned grass-cutter mechanic, Paul Meadows. Then her mind turned to thoughts of Crawford Arrowsmith, the way she had known it would the moment she was alone.

There was nothing she could do about her discovery that she loved him—it was there for all time. No amount of telling herself he was the most infuriating, overbearing brute she had ever met, a man she had started out hating, could alter the fact that the reason for those odd sensations she had felt time and again when she was with him had been a mischievous Cupid telling her that her hatred of him was just a cover for a deeper, more powerful emotion.

The sound of the lawnmower starting up had her going to the window to see the twins being scooped up into safety. Whatever had been wrong with the lawnmower had been put right, and she saw that Paul Meadows was cutting the grass she hadn't yet been able to summon up the strength to tackle. Teddy was standing watching him, and it looked such a perfect family scene she felt her heart lurch within her, so that she had to come away from the window and sit down on her bed.

She felt no jealousy that she had no part in the scene she had just witnessed. If anything grew out of what she had just seen, and she was prepared to accept that having found herself in love she might be imagining a growing warmth between the two out there where none existed, she would be pleased. It was just that for a moment she had pictured herself out there with Crawford mowing a lawn they both shared, while she kept an eye open for any mischief her own babies, hers and Crawford's, might get up to.

Presently she got up off the bed. Oh, to think of the way she had responded to him! Her face flamed at the remembrance of it. She'd asked for all she'd got. Vividly Crawford's voice came back to her, his saying he had no intention of seducing her. 'I just never expected to have so much co-operation,' he had said. Oh where had the cool, calm P.A. been then? Unable to bear the agony of embarrassed thoughts, Gerry brushed her hair and quickly escaped from the quietness of the room.

It was much better downstairs; at least she was able to occupy herself. She hurried round preparing a meal, her feet flying as she raced from pantry to kitchen to dining table as though trying to outstrip the thoughts that dived in on her when she was determined not to think at all. She slowed down when she heard the others coming, and moved away from the sink when Paul Meadows came in with Teddy to wash his hands.

'Thanks for doing that job,' Gerry said. 'I fully intended to cut the grass this week but never got round to it.'

'My pleasure,' Paul told her, the familiar twinkle in his eyes beaming in her direction, covering the fact he was also running a professional eye over her. 'Actually Teddy had the same idea when I called, and was already wielding your piece of antique machinery with the same expertise as I imagine she would use with a combine harvester when I arrived.'

Gerry looked at Teddy to see how she was taking this piece of teasing. Teddy didn't seem about to retaliate in kind as she half expected, but just looked at Paul as he turned to her, and smiled. Gerry looked away. There had been a friendly intimacy in that look that made her feel an intruder. It was a brief look, but long enough for Gerry to know that even if these two people didn't know it yet themselves, Cupid was ready to have a go at them too.

She turned away, and as Paul had left the sink and was now drying his hands, took his place and turned on the cold water tap and started to fill up the bowl—though with no idea what reason she had for doing so.

'How are you feeling, Miss Barton?' She came to to hear Paul addressing her, and turned off the tap and upended the bowl.

'Gerry,' she said, realising since she was his patient, where Teddy wasn't, perhaps ethics made him unlikely to call her by her first name. Dr Bidley always called her Gerry, but he was old enough to be her father. 'I'm fine— I was coming to see you tonight to say I'm going back to work on Monday.'

Paul shook his head doubtfully. 'I don't think so, Gerry. Give it another week.' He could see from her expression she didn't like the idea. 'Your employer would bring the G.M.C. down on me if he had to bring you home from work in the same condition as last time,' he told her, trying to lighten her expression.

Since Paul had no idea what had transpired between her and Crawford that afternoon, Gerry forced a smile to hide her feelings. 'All right,' she agreed. 'But I can definitely return to work the week after, can't I?'

'We'll see,' said Paul noncommittally.

When she thought about it afterwards, Gerry came to think perhaps it was just as well she wasn't going back to work on Monday. She didn't know how she was going to face Crawford for one thing—and the longer she left returning to the office, the more likelihood there was of William Hudson, her new boss, being in the chair. She knew for certain Crawford would never again call at the cottage, and felt sick every time she thought of the cold way he had left her after he had brought her home from that drive—he had hardly waited to see her out of the car before he had roared away.

It was in the middle of the following week that Gerry elected to leave Teddy catching up on the ever-present pile of washing, while she took Emma and Sarah for an outing. She had been out for about an hour, and turned the corner into the road where they lived and could have sworn she saw Crawford's car driving away up the hill. It wasn't the convertible but the saloon model he used.

Her first feeling was of disappointment that she had missed seeing him. Then as commonsense homed in, she was glad—if indeed it had been him—that she had missed him. She couldn't think why he should call—could have sworn he would give Little Layton as wide a berth as possible, and knew she would have gone scarlet if it had been she who had answered his knock on the door.

Unconsciously, her feet had quickened their pace; they seemed to know what she wasn't ready to admit, that she wanted to get to the cottage as quickly as possible to find out what Crawford had been doing in Little Layton. As far as she knew they were the only people in the village he knew—and he wouldn't come in the middle of a busy working day just for the ride.

'Was that Crawford's car I just saw?' Gerry asked her sister without preamble as soon as she was inside the back door.

'Er ...' Teddy blushed, and made a job of rinsing out the last of the nappies.

'You've gone red,' Gerry said with sisterly candour. 'What did he want?' She was sure now it had been him—and witnessed with growing disquiet the colour staining her sister's cheeks. Teddy never blushed unless she had been found out in something she had been up to.

'Er—it's meant to be a surprise,' Teddy said, recovering her composure.

Oh God, he's asked her to marry him, Gerry thought for no logical reason, and knew she just wouldn't be able to take being his sister-in-law.

'What is?' She made her voice sound calm and disinterested, while her fingernails bit into her palms as she waited.

'Crawford's had your car repaired—it's being delivered tomorrow.'

'Oh!' All that sank in was the fact that her worst fears hadn't been realised. 'That was nice of him.' Nothing she tried could put any warmth into her voice—she felt frozen inside at the torment of her emotions, and said anything to get off the subject of Crawford. 'The twins' pushchair doesn't squeak any more,' she said it as if it was news she didn't think Teddy could wait to hear.

Teddy looked her in the eyes then for the first time, only Gerry had been too tense to notice she had been avoiding looking at her. 'I know,' she said. 'Paul oiled it.'

It was Gerry's turn the next morning to rinse through a few of the children's things while Teddy took the twins out. Most times when Gerry wasn't working, they went out together, but Teddy had said yesterday she didn't feel like a walk, and today Gerry wanted to be in when the A35 was delivered.

She still couldn't weigh up why Crawford had called personally with the message when he could easily have telephoned. But after a lot of thinking about it, she came to the conclusion that he must have been going in the general direction of Little Layton, and had decided Honeysuckle Cottage wasn't too far out of his way. She could well have gone herself to collect it, she mused—it would probably not have taken too long since a bus went from the village at half past nine, and she would have no need to wait hours for another bus back—but still, she had to concede, having her tyre mended and having the car delivered back to her had been more than she could have expected since Crawford had no opinion at all of her.

Mrs Chapman came in from where she had been busily occupied in the living room, bringing Gerry's thoughts away from Crawford for a brief while—though not for long, since it seemed impossible to get him out of her mind these days. She would have to do something about that soon, but what, she had no idea. She couldn't afford to leave a job that paid so well—though when he went back to London she wouldn't see him again ...

'We've run out of polish,' Mrs Chapman brought her back to earth.

'I'll get some when I go shopping tomorrow,' Gerry promised with a smile, and heard how Mrs Chapman's mother used to make her own polish with vinegar and paraffin. Then in the same breath Mrs Chapman said she would pop up and 'do' upstairs.

After Mrs Chapman had gone upstairs Gerry reflected over the conversation she'd had with her soon after Teddy had gone out. Conversation, she mused, was hardly the word to describe the few sentences that had passed between them when she had told her she would be paying her wages from now on.

'Oh, but Mr Arrowsmith's paid me to the end of the month,' Mrs Chapman stated, seeing nothing wrong in the arrangement, apparently. 'He said he'd send me a cheque at the beginning of next month too—I haven't got a bank, but our June will change it for me—he's nice, isn't he, Mr Arrowsmith. A lovely man.'

Gerry could hear Mrs Chapman moving the furniture about upstairs, and went into the living room to see if there were any signs of her car coming. She was going to pay him back somehow, she determined. Somehow he was going to be made to take his money back. As yet she wasn't sure how this was going to be achieved since the last time she had attempted to do just that he had very nearly broken her wrist—well, perhaps that was a bit of an exaggeration, but she'd certainly had bruises for a day or two.

She was in the kitchen when her car was delivered, so didn't see it arrive, but the sounds of car doors being closed had her going out to investigate. The sight that met her eyes was enough to make her cry, but she fought back the tears and went to greet the two men who had delivered a shining A35 to her door. Her car was parked on the drive, and a van with Arrowsmith Electronics emblazoned on the side was parked by the kerb, the van driver having followed her car and now ready to take the other man back.

'Not bad, eh?' the older, shorter of the two men greeted

her as he saw her eyes riveted in disbelief on the car that had been rusty, battered, dented, and held together more by prayer than by anything else.

'What have you done to it?' she gasped, unable to believe the evidence of her own eyes. For in place of the old wreck she had pointed out to Crawford that day he had brought her home was a shining, immaculate A35, with not a dent in it.

'We had orders from the top to strip it down, report on it, and after that to build it up again.' He then went on to tell her about the worn-out track rod ends and king-pins, talked some more about brake cylinders and shoes—all of which meant very little to Gerry and wouldn't have sunk in anyway, for her eyes were still glued to the car which was shining so brightly, she couldn't help but think it had been re-sprayed as well.

She was sure of it as she went to take a closer look, and said as much, and had her suspicions confirmed, plus further talk of welding and undersealing.

'I was told to tell you to give it a trial run before you drive it into town,' the short man told her. 'The steering will be spot on now, so you'll have to adjust to that.' Gerry remembered there had been quite a bit of play in the steering before, and thanked the man wholeheartedly, since it became obvious he had done the majority of the work. 'It was a treat to do it,' he said, looking well pleased himself. 'It was a good little car in its day.'

The two men went off down the path, only for the man who had done most of the talking to come hurrying back again. 'Nearly forgot,' he said, holding out a slip of paper. 'Your M.O.T. certificate. You'll be all right now for twelve months—though you shouldn't have any trouble getting another seventy-thousand miles out of her now.'

Gerry couldn't bear to think of the cost of restoring her car to its new pristine condition. She was already in Crawford's debt over Mrs Chapman—hadn't yet been able to come up with a way of settling that account, though she had thought vaguely of sending him a cheque with a polite note repeating what she had already told him, that she would pay Mrs Chapman herself from now on. But now here she was landed with a bill she could never hope to repay—it must run into hundreds since the mechanic had talked of new wings and various other parts. Crawford might think he had been doing her a favour, and she had to admit he had settled a very pressing problem that had been worrying her of how she was going to get to and from work on Monday—but it was against all her instincts to owe money. Something threatened to rise up and choke her at the thought of being in his debt. She sought through her mind for something to sell—there wasn't anything.

The joy of seeing her car, so lovely, so immaculate, had disappeared. It didn't help when Teddy came in with every appearance of having been on a spending spree in the few stores the village possessed.

'I couldn't resist these little T-shirts for the twins— aren't they gorgeous?' she enthused. 'And while I was in the chemist, I bought us both a lipstick.'

CHAPTER NINE

GERRY'S first day back at work was much less traumatic than she had been building herself up for. Ever since she had awakened that morning there had been one thought and one thought only in her mind—how on earth was she going to face Crawford again? That it had to be done, that there was no way she could get out of it, had been with her almost continuously since the last time she had parted from him. To tell herself he would have gone back to London by now, would have no need to visit the Layton branch of his company except for the occasional conference with the higher up executives, didn't ring true in her ears. She knew instinctively that as sure as night followed day, some time sooner or later she was going to come up against him, and she couldn't make up her mind whether she wanted to get it over and done with today or whether a few more weeks of not seeing him might ease the pain of that meeting.

'Oh no!' wailed Teddy, sitting up in bed and watching while Gerry dressed her hair. 'Not that style again, love— it does nothing for you.'

Gerry continued to work her hair into its bun. She didn't like it either, but felt better able to adopt the cool front she thought necessary to get her through the day if *he* was there.

'You're only jealous because yours isn't long enough to do the same,' she kidded Teddy, whose own hair had been cut short and professionally curled on Saturday.

'Phooey!'

For all Teddy hadn't said as she had in the past, 'Don't be home late, will you,' Gerry parked her car in its usual spot ready for a quick getaway and walked smartly along the pavements to Arrowsmith's. She was almost at the swing doors before Basil Dyer caught up with her.

'Better?' he asked, his pleasant face smiling a welcome. 'I've missed you around the place.' Basil would have said more, in fact he looked all set to give her the lowdown on the gossip she had missed since being away, but someone else attracted his attention, and she left him in conversation on the ground floor and made her way up the stairs. It was nice of him to say he had missed her around the place, it made her feel more like a person and less of a number.

As she turned into the corridor that housed her own office, her footsteps hesitated and came to a faltering stop outside the door she was to go through. She heard footsteps coming along the corridor behind her, which effectively made up her mind for her—anyone who had any business being on this floor would wonder what she was doing hovering outside her own office door.

It was a huge anti-climax to have built herself up to go through the door, only to find both offices empty. Relief vied with disappointment, and as Gerry sank down on to her chair behind her desk, she determined she would never let herself become so keyed up again—her legs felt quite weak and she had to take her handkerchief from her bag to deal with her moist palms.

The snap of the door handle being turned had her eyes riveted to it, tension again flooding through her, only to leave her fighting to look natural when a stocky man of about forty came through the door.

'You must be Geraldine Barton,' he said, coming into the room and holding out his hand. She liked his easy smile, she thought, as he introduced himself. 'I'm William Hudson—I like my coffee black and my tea sweet.' Gerry had to smile in answer; he had an infectious way with him. She stamped down on the sudden panicky feeling that she might never see Crawford again, for all she had only moments earlier been dreading exactly that. 'That takes care of the priorities,' William Hudson gave her no time for further thought. 'Would you like to come through to my office and we'll see what's to be done—though knowing my cousin I'm sure everything will be in apple pie order.'

Her first day back turned out to be quite pleasant. During the day she learned that William Hudson with his wife, two sons and a daughter had moved from London last week. Learned that he had visited the Layton branch on previous occasions and already knew most of the senior executives, though one or two stopped by during the day to make him welcome. Although none of his visitors stayed very long, the interruption of their calling, together with the fact of William's newness to the job, for all she thought he was as capable and decidedly more efficient than Mr Gillett, meant that they were nowhere near finished as the hands of the clock neared five.

In two minds whether or not to ring Teddy and tell her she would be late, Gerry's train of thought was interrupted by William glancing at his watch.

'You'd better get off now, Gerry,' he said, looking at her with his easy smile, having no difficulty in shortening her name. 'Crawford made a point of telling me you were not to work overtime.'

Gerry wanted to protest, wanted to say she didn't want any favours from Crawford—wasn't she already too far in his debt? But a picture of Teddy watching for her from the window flashed through her mind, and she gave in without a fight, except to say, 'Are you sure?' her eyes falling to the calculations she had been checking with him.

'Positive.' Again the sunny smile. 'You wouldn't want me to be nailed to the yard-arm on my first day, would you—there's nothing here that can't wait until tomorrow.'

Now that she was getting used to the A35—it had seemed as though she was driving a totally different car at first—Gerry quite enjoyed the drive home. She prepared to wave to Teddy as she slowed down to turn on to the drive, but for once Teddy wasn't there.

Gerry found her in the kitchen, and to her surprise discovered that her sister seemed to have lost her fretful anxiety at being on her own for most of the day. Mrs Chapman's company must be a help, of course, she thought, as she greeted her twin before going to say hello to her two nieces.

'Is it that time already?' Teddy sounded so cheerful, bubbling over, so like she had been in the old days that Gerry had to turn away so she shouldn't see the light of gladness for her in her eyes. 'How did your first day go—has it taken the stuffing out of you?'

'No, it was fine. My new boss has arrived.'

'You haven't see Crawford today?'

Gerry told her she hadn't, and edged to the living room to take a peep at Emma and Sarah who had been happily enough occupied until they had seen their aunt, but who now raised their arms, both wanting to be picked up at once.

With one child apiece, Teddy told her she could tell her about her new boss over their meal. 'I've some exciting news of my own,' she said, looking down at the child on her hip, whose dimpled hand was bent on investigating her hair.

Gerry looked at her enquiringly, but Teddy was busily engaged in untangling Sarah's fingers. Then Emma decided to copy her sister, and for the next couple of hours they were kept busy with the needs of the children.

Knowing Teddy of old, Gerry knew there was no point in pressing her to tell her what her exciting news was. As a child Teddy had been prone to keep everyone on edge until the last moment, building up the drama until she could no longer keep it to herself. Tonight, though, Gerry had a suspicion that the news Teddy had to reveal was being kept back because she had no idea how to go about telling her what it was. She thought of several things it might be that Teddy had to tell her, but none of them could be termed 'exciting', except the one thing that came to mind again and again, and that was that Teddy's news was connected with the friendship she had witnessed growing between her sister and Paul Meadows. She might be jumping the gun, and of course it was early days yet, but Paul could have called today while she was out at work.

She was certain suddenly that it was something to do with Paul and her sister was perhaps a little shy to tell her, for all she had never suspected Teddy of being shy, while admitting that love did funny things to one. Look at how her own thoughts had gone haywire since she had discovered her love for Crawford. She decided it would only need a gentle prodding word and all Teddy's news would come flowing out in a rush.

'Shall we talk about your news, Ted, or do you want to hear about my William Hudson? I'll confess I'd rather hear your news first.'

Their meal over, Teddy selected an apple from the fruit bowl and carefully began to peel it. 'I've come into some money,' she said after a few moments.

Just like that—she hadn't dressed it up. Just a bald statement giving no indication of whether it was five pence or five pounds, or even from whom she had come into it.

'Where ... who ...?' They had been hard up for so long, and Teddy's statement had been the last thing she had been expecting to hear.

Having got started on the subject. Teddy was no longer reticent in telling Gerry the rest of it. Gerry learned, her eyes growing wider and wider, that some time last month Teddy had sent a relative of Mark's a photograph of the twins, and had received a letter back inviting her and the twins to stay for a while. Teddy had written back saying the expense of making the visit had been beyond their means—and today a cheque had arrived for five hundred pounds.

'Five hundred pounds!' Gerry repeated in astonishment, unable to take it in. 'You did say five hundred pounds?'

Teddy confirmed that she had, and went on enthusiastically to say how they could all have new clothes. 'It'll be marvellous, Gerry, won't it—after all the scrimping and saving, to be able to go into any store we like and buy just what we want. We could buy a washing machine if we wanted—I'm so fed up doing all the washing by hand. I know you do your fair share of it,' she amended hastily, as in all honesty she was bound to do.

Gerry secretly thought a washing machine would make a big hole in the five hundred pounds, but it wasn't in her

to take the light out of Teddy's face. It was the first time
her sister had mentioned scrimping and saving. She had
tried her best not to let Teddy see how carefully she
worked out their budget, though she guessed now Teddy
must have caught a glimpse of one of her many tottings up,
since they not only shared the same cottage, but the same
bedroom too. They talked for some while about the money
till Gerry remarked:

'I didn't know Mark had any relatives still living, much
less that you'd sent off a picture of Emma and Sarah.' She
had thought Mark had been brought up in a children's
home. She was sure Teddy had told her there had not
been one solitary relative able to take him in when his
parents had been killed, but she must have been mistaken.

'Oh yes, I knew he had this great-aunt. I'd forgotten
about her myself, actually, then when we had that lovely
picture of the twins taken—you know the one,' she said,
and described a snap taken in the garden not so long ago,
which Gerry had to admit was a delightful picture of them.
'Well, I suppose my motherly instinct reared up and I
wanted to show off to someone.'

Gerry smiled at her understandingly. She knew exactly
how Teddy felt. She'd wanted to take that snap to the
office—had thought of showing it to Basil Dyer thinking
that since he was so happy with his own children he might
be interested to see it, only of course, since no one at
Arrowsmith's had known of her home circumstances, she
had thought better of it.

'Anyway,' Teddy went on, 'you know how we value the
privacy of our correspondence—and I wasn't sure if the old
dear was still at the address I wrote to, so I didn't say
anything.'

Gerry acknowledged without rancour what Teddy was
saying. They had been brought up to regard each other's
letters as private, and she'd always agreed that a letter
from one person to another deserved the right to be private

and not looked at by anyone other than the person it was intended for. She couldn't help a small feeling of wanting to see the letter from Mark's great-aunt, though, but Teddy had effectively blocked that wish by reminding her of the value of private correspondence.

By the end of the evening they had decided they would set off as early as the twins would allow on Saturday morning, and take the Layton storekeepers by storm. On a laughing note they went to bed, Teddy barely able to wait for Saturday morning to arrive, and Gerry thinking how completely wrong she had been with her thoughts of her sister and Paul Meadows.

Half way through the following morning Gerry looked up to find William Hudson standing before her, his face showing a little boy smile, which denoted, Gerry thought, that he wanted something and was half ashamed to ask for it.

'Does going and fetching me a packet of smokes come into the duties of P.A.?' he asked. 'I've run out and I'm expecting a phone call any minute.'

'Which brand?' Gerry asked easily, rising from her chair.

On the way back she bumped smack, bang into Robin as she turned round one of the corners. Since their relationship at one time had been so close, though looking at him now she began to wonder what she had ever seen as so wonderful about him—he didn't bear comparison with Crawford—she felt she couldn't very well just walk straight past him.

'Are you better?' he asked, seeming only to wait until she told him she was, before he was telling her he had been ill. 'Had 'flu,' he went on. 'My first day back.'

He didn't look too well even now, Gerry thought, as she commiserated with him. But then from what she could remember of him he never did have a very good colour, and she paused to think herself very fickle to have forgotten so much about him when she had thought at one time of living out the rest of her years with him. The idea made her shiver involuntarily, and she smiled to cover it —there was only one man for her, and she might as well plan her next holiday on the moon for all the chance there was of Crawford ever returning her feelings.

'I intended to get in touch with you before I went sick,' he told her. 'But no one seemed to know where you lived, and Personnel guard their files as if they suspect the K.G.B. are after them.'

Robin's conversation, his seeming not to be content with the two of them being a couple of people who just happened to work for the same company, had her seeking for an excuse to get away from him.

'I must dash, Robin,' she said, brandishing the cigarettes she had just purchased. 'My boss is gasping for these.'

Robin made a protesting movement as she made her getaway. She didn't turn around, and hoped he had got the message that she was not interested in renewing their friendship.

The door to William's office was closed when she got back, but knowing he hadn't any appointments fixed for that morning, she didn't think twice about opening the door and going through. But once there, she stopped dead, and a riot of colour flooded her cheeks, forcing her to grip tightly on to her self-control as she saw the tall, athletic figure of Crawford Arrowsmith come away from the window. She knew he had fixed his sights on her, but she felt incapable of looking at him after that first glance, and without a word, feeling too choked to speak, she placed the cigarettes she had purchased, together with the change, on the desk in front of William, and turned to make her escape, with William's, 'You're an angel, Gerry,' following her through the door.

Back at her desk she fought to regain her self-control. Idiot, idiot, she berated herself. Why couldn't she have tossed him a casual 'Good morning'? He hadn't spoken to her either, admittedly. Not that she'd given him much chance, merely dropped the cigarettes and change on the desk and bolted.

She was glad Crawford was taking some time talking to his cousin. It gave her precious time to collect herself together, gave her time to don her 'touch-me-not' air. When Crawford came through that door, as indeed he must—unless she was lucky enough to be at lunch when he came out and went, she hoped, back to London—she wanted to be fully in charge and mistress of her wayward emotions.

As the time went on she found herself listening for sounds coming from the other room that would denote that the door would shortly open, and tensed a dozen times only to find herself mistaken. There were two jobs of equal importance she could do—one was to check through a file for some information William wanted, the other was a batch of typing. She opted to type. Should Crawford elect to say a few words as he passed her desk—though she secretly doubted he had anything he wanted to say to her after the way they had last parted—then she wouldn't give him the opportunity to say very much. He was hardly the kind who would stand and yell over the noise of the typewriter.

The door opened just as she was rolling a fresh sheet of paper into her machine. She knew without looking up that it was Crawford, and gave her full concentration to straightening up the paper. It was unnerving being in the same room and not one word being spoken, but since he obviously had nothing to say, she wasn't going to be the first one to speak. She felt rather than heard him move, and felt her muscles tighten as he came to the back of her to stand behind her chair.

Then all her nerves gathered together in one jangling alarm system, for she felt his hands in her hair, and one by one he was removing the pins from her neat bun.

'What are you doing?' was jerked out of her as she spun round on her chair, feeling her hair falling about her shoulders.

'So you do have a tongue?' Those slate grey eyes didn't seem at all put out by her furious expression. 'I thought we'd progressed past the schoolmarm image.'

If that was an oblique reference to the way she had responded to his lovemaking, Gerry knew, as a fresh surge of colour rioted through her face, she just wasn't up to getting involved in answering remarks of that kind, and she'd have thought anyway that he would have preferred to forget the whole episode.

'I don't like my hair loose at the office,' she said after a few moments when it seemed he had nothing further to add, appearing quite content to prop himself on the corner of her desk and admire his handiwork.

'I do,' was his brief comment as he stood up. 'Leave it the way it is.' It wasn't so much a request as an order, and instinctively her rebellious spirit had her hands going to her hair, her eyes on the pins he had extracted and laid on the desk in front of her.

His eyes followed hers, and if he read the thought in her mind that as soon as he had gone those pins would again be securing a neat if unbecoming bun, he couldn't have thwarted her intention more easily. In one movement every one of the pins had been scooped up and were resting in his pocket before her hand could reach them.

'I said leave it.' His eyes hadn't missed the spark of anger at his action, but it didn't seem to bother him, for his glance went from her eyes, moved to her mouth, and smiled as though recalling pleasant memories, before returning to hold her eyes once more. What he said next was the last thing she expected him to say, for he took her completely unawares, seeming impervious to the fact that she was angry with him.

'Come and have dinner with me tonight.'

'I can't.' Her reply had been quick and without thought. It sounded blunt, she knew, as it sank in that Crawford was actually inviting her to have dinner with him.

'Why can't you? Or is it that you don't want to?'

It was no news to her that Crawford didn't easily take no for an answer, but this time he was going to have to. Apart from the fact she had nothing decent to wear that could do justice to the occasion of dining with the man who unknown to him had stolen her heart, she couldn't leave Teddy on her own. And the implication of what his dinner invitation really meant sank in, that he was aware how easy it was for him to get her to respond to him—hadn't he just referred to it in a roundabout way? She knew that love him she might, but she had no intention of being just a passing affair.

'I never go out at night,' she told him, and saw the beginnings of frost appear in his eyes, for all his mouth was smiling.

'Then it's about time you damn well did,' he said, and she wasn't at all deceived by his mild tone.

She knew she had irritated him. He probably thought she'd be a pushover for his charm—well, she was. If he knew how much her nerves were jangling at this very moment he would have no doubt about it. His tone altered slightly, a persuasive note entering that had her weakening when she knew she shouldn't.

'Come on, Gerry,' he cajoled. 'I give you my word I won't seduce you if that's what's worrying you.'

It seemed incidental to tell him he wouldn't get the chance. He would know that was pure bravado talking—since he'd got her into such a state the last time he'd kissed her she had buttoned up her dress with ten thumbs. She looked into his slate grey eyes, not wanting to give in, but owning at last that she was too much in love with him to let thoughts of Teddy deny her this one evening.

'Mrs Chapman can sit with your sister, if you're anxious about leaving her on her own.' His tone was quite gentle now, understanding even. But at the mention of Mrs Chapman's name, all her deserted wits came rushing back. Storming home came the remembrance of how much she owed him, how much she was in his debt—how unlikely it was she would ever get out of his debt.

Tearing her eyes away from his, she looked down at her desk. 'I don't want to dine with you,' she said, and couldn't help that her refusal was blunt to the point of rudeness, because this conversation had to be terminated, and now. She mustn't give him another chance to work on the crumbling foundations of her will power.

What he would have said, she didn't know. Perhaps he wouldn't have said anything. Perhaps her refusal to dine with him didn't bother him anyway, but just at that moment the telephone on her desk bleeped to be answered, and she was never more glad of the interruption, as still without looking at Crawford, she lifted the phone off its rest to answer it.

It was an internal call. And when she heard Robin's voice at the other end, in an attempt to make Crawford believe she was in no way affected by him—for he showed no inclination to leave her office—Gerry's voice was a shade warmer than it might otherwise have been.

'Hello, Robin,' she said eagerly, her voice sounding as though she hadn't seen him for months instead of the hour or so ago it had been in the corridor.

'I didn't say a quarter or an eighth of what I wanted to say to you, Gerry,' Robin's voice came back, sounding warm in return. 'I wondered if we could meet somewhere —it's impossible to talk in this place ...'

Robin was going on to suggest where they could meet that evening, and Gerry was overwhelmingly conscious of the stillness of Crawford standing not a yard away from her, ready to listen to every word of her side of the conversation.

'Why don't you come to supper?' she found herself saying, when it was the last thing she wanted to say.

'Will Teddy be there?'

'Of course.'

'Then if you don't mind, I won't.' So he still had this thing about Teddy. She refused to let it rattle her while Crawford was taking in every word. She hadn't asked *him* to supper—nor did he have a thing about Teddy, though she doubted he would have accepted anyway. 'How about lunch today—since you aren't taking up any of my offers for an evening date?'

She must have missed that part of his conversation in her attempt not to overplay her hand with Crawford there. 'That would be lovely—what time?'

'Five past one outside the main entrance?'

'I'll look forward to it,' she was saying as the door from her office into the corridor slammed shut, as Crawford left.

She badly wanted to cry after she'd put down the phone. Crawford would never again ask her out to dinner—not after the way she had refused his invitation and before the breath of her refusal had cooled, straightaway, and in Crawford's presence, invited another man into her home. She didn't cry, told herself she had done the only thing possible. She knew she should feel glad at Robin's timely phone call, but far from looking forward to seeing Robin again, she knew she couldn't wait for two o'clock when she would be back at her desk again.

Robin was waiting for her when she pushed through the swing doors just after one, his pale face lighting up when he saw her.

'Glad to see you've let your hair down,' he said, giving her a smile that at one time would have thrilled her but now left her cold, as she realised he thought she had taken the pins out of her hair for his benefit.

He took her to a cafeteria not far away, and although it was crowded at this time of day, they managed to find a small table for two squashed up in a corner. While Robin downed beans on toast and Gerry drank her soup, Robin filled her in on what he had been doing in the time since they had parted. The job in Birmingham hadn't come up to his expectations, he told her, coupled with which he had missed her more than he had thought he would. He had tried to stick it out, but when he had seen a job advertised at Arrowsmiths he had applied and been accepted for it. He had been overjoyed on his first day there to hear her name mentioned as the P.A. to the Mr Gillett who had left under a cloud.

'You were in London at the time,' he reminded her. 'But I came to see you the first day you were back.' He didn't mention how shocked he had been at how she had changed, but went on, 'When you fainted, Mr Arrowsmith ordered me out, and as I said this morning, I tried to find out where you lived, but nobody seemed to know—then I went down with this rotten summer 'flu. I was quite ill,' he said reflectively. 'Anyhow,' he resumed, 'now we're together again, and I wanted to tell you my feelings for you haven't changed, Gerry.'

Gerry concentrated on her empty soup bowl. She'd known all along that she shouldn't have come. It hadn't been fair on Robin to give him even the small encouragement of having lunch with him. Her circumstances hadn't changed—there was still Teddy and the twins to be looked after. Any plans Robin had for her in his scheme of things didn't include Teddy, she knew that without having to ask, and it seemed like hitting below the belt to mention it, since she had no intention of their relationship ever going any further.

'I'm sorry, Robin,' she said quietly. There was no way she could dress it up. 'I—my feelings for you have changed.'

She was back at her desk before two. Robin had not

been very happy at what she'd told him. He had seen her acceptance of his offer to lunch as encouragement, as she had suspected too late he would. There had been a stiff silence between them as they walked back to the office, and Gerry had been unable to think of anything to say to break it—and with Robin looking the way he had, she was sure he wouldn't have answered her anyway.

William Hudson returned from his own lunch shortly afterwards, and paused by her desk for a few moments and they exchanged a few pleasantries prior to him continuing through to his own room. Gerry asked him if he was anywhere near straight at home, remembering it had taken an age to get everything shipshape at the cottage when she and Teddy had moved.

'Another ten years should sort out the chaos,' he exaggerated on a grand scale. 'Though the main rooms are clear—bedrooms too,' he added as an afterthought. 'We've even got one of the guest rooms sorted,' he mused out loud. 'I thought Crawford might want a place to doss down other than a hotel when he comes to Layton and stays overnight. But he always was a loner, and I can't say I blame him for preferring to put up at the Creighton House,' he said, naming a hotel just outside Layton that was well known locally for its service, cuisine and, Gerry thought, its high cost. 'My family seem to have a crisis every other day,' he confessed, smiling as though he took his family crises all in his stride. 'Well, I must get on—Crawford's a hard taskmaster and I get no special treatment just because we happen to be related.'

Gerry reflected when he'd gone that William hadn't got the job of Company Secretary just because of his blood tie with the head of Arrowsmiths. He had told her himself with the easy way he had with him, that he had had to apply formally along with all the other candidates for the job.

On Saturday, as arranged, with Teddy sitting in the

back of the A35, Emma and Sarah either side of her, their pushchair in the boot and with Gerry driving, they went into Layton to shop.

Gerry could see her sister was enjoying every moment of it as she bought three dresses without hesitation, lingerie and shoes for herself, new outfits for the twins, plus two frothy bits of nonsense that were babies' dresses, which cost the earth, wouldn't last five minutes, and had nothing to recommend them except Teddy's opinion that, 'They'll look simply gorgeous in these.' Gerry smiled affectionately at her sister, realising how much it meant to be able to spend without counting the cost.

But when Teddy insisted she also should have something new, she demurred. 'The money was sent for you, Ted, not me,' she said gently, not wanting to upset her happy day.

'Phooey!' said Teddy, using her favourite expression when she didn't think there was anything to argue over.

'But Mark's great-aunt would be upset if she knew you were spending her money to buy clothes for me,' Gerry felt bound to protest, and felt uncomfortable as Teddy fixed her with one of her 'I'm the elder sister' looks.

'Don't spoil the day for me, love,' she said, making Gerry feel awful. 'You've spent enough on us in the past—do you want me to start feeling guilty about that?'

'Oh, Teddy, no!' Instantly Gerry was won over, and didn't see her sister's satisfied grin at her piece of emotional blackmail.

Gerry chose a brown linen skirt and waistcoat and matched them with a creamy-coloured shirt to go underneath, which she thought would do very nicely for the office. And at Teddy's insistence that the silky dress in a lovely silver-grey shade must have been made specially for her—its large sleeves emphasising her delicate wrists, the fitted bodice making the most of her average sized but firm bust, and the way it swung in gores with every movement round her calves, and in view of Teddy's remarks about making her feel guilty, Gerry accepted that dress too.

'It's the sort of dress you can wear during the day and in the evening when we entertain,' Teddy said, and they both burst out laughing as each had the same thought. 'I know,' said Teddy, once they had sobered, 'we never entertain, do we?' It was lovely to see Teddy laughing, Gerry thought.

Shortly after that the twins became restive. 'It's pointless looking at washing machines now,' Teddy stated, shushing Emma who had become bored and let out a wail in the middle of the store that had all heads turning in their direction. 'Anyone would think I'm murdering her,' Teddy muttered. It didn't help that Sarah decided she wanted to air her vocal cords too.

'Come on, Ted,' Gerry urged. 'Let's get home—I'll pick up some washing machine pamphlets in my lunch hour on Monday.'

Monday got off to a bad start. Dressed in her new skirt, matching waistcoat and shirt, Gerry sat before the dressing table mirror, her hand stretching out for the new supply of hairpins she had bought.

'Don't,' Teddy's voice from behind her stayed her hand.

'No?' Gerry questioned. She liked the way she looked in her new outfit, the weight she'd gained and managed to hold on to suited her, and she secretly thought it a pity to spoil the whole effect by screwing her hair back, but . . .

'Definitely no,' said Teddy, shaking her head from side to side.

'All right,' Gerry began, when a bloodcurdling cry came from next door.

Gerry was first into the twins' room. Teddy not far behind her was in time to see Gerry extracting a tearful Sarah from her cot. 'Give her to me,' Teddy said practically. 'She's damp both ends by the look of her—you don't want to ruin your outfit. What was all that about?' she asked, as she soothed the tearful Sarah.

'I think she jammed her fingers in the cot fastener.'

They both examined Sarah's prying finger, and saw it was a little red. 'Paul might pop in later, I'll get him to take at look at it,' said Teddy, obviously without thinking, because she went a little pink as she realised what she'd said, then added with a touch of aggression that was pure Teddy when she felt she was being backed into a corner, 'He sometimes calls for a cup of tea.'

'Good for him,' Gerry said mildly, and grinned. 'I like Paul—he's nice.'

'Yes—well, you're going to be late,' said Teddy, who rarely bothered what time her sister arrived at work.

Gerry was late—ten minutes. And she had no valid excuse either, she thought as she pushed through the swing doors of Arrowsmiths. Sarah's accident had taken no more than a few minutes to attend to. The clock at home must be losing again, she thought as she glanced at the huge clock in the foyer, unable to believe it said ten past nine. She made for the lifts—not so busy now—and in a minute or so was at the door of her office. She didn't think William would mind about her lateness—she would make up the time in her lunch hour. It had gone half past nine a couple of mornings last week when he had come in, though what time he finished at night she never knew, because he insisted she leave the office bang on time.

It was not William Hudson she saw as she pushed open the door, but Crawford. Instantly she veiled her eyes as she threw a cool 'Good morning' in his general direction, and went to seat herself behind her desk, wondering at the same time whether he had driven himself down from London this morning or if he had stayed in Layton over the weekend. She couldn't think that Layton had very much to offer him in the way of entertainment, and felt a scorching jealousy sear through her as she pictured some lovely female keeping him amused.

'Bad night with the twins?'

Gerry looked up, not quite with him for a moment, then decided he was referring to the fact of her late arrival. He was looking at her as if he liked what he saw, and she felt warm colour flood through her as his eyes flicked over her figure-hugging waistcoat.

'Er—no—the clock was wrong.'

She veiled her eyes again, feeling her nerves beginning to fray. She wished William would hurry up and come. And then she forgot all about William, for without her knowing, Crawford had moved and was beside her and bending towards her.

'You know the penalty for being late,' he said smoothly, and before it could register what he was about to do, she felt his warm lips taking hers in a brief but mind-stultifying possession. Even while the words 'Don't do that', were rising up to be spoken, he had moved away and was saying coolly, 'I like the outfit—it suits you.'

'It's new.'

Gerry wished she hadn't said that—far better ignore him. It was as though she was telling him she hadn't had anything new for ages, and now that she had, she wanted everybody to know about it. Feeling embarrassed, she flicked a glance at him, but if he thought her announcement was gauche or immature, it didn't show in his face. If anything, he looked as if the idea of her treating herself to some new clothes pleased him—though why it should she couldn't fathom, unless he was fed up seeing her around the office in her ill-fitting clothes.

William Hudson coming in took all speculations on what Crawford's look had been all about from her mind. 'Morning, Crawford—morning, Gerry,' and turning back to Crawford they both sauntered into the other office, William's voice reaching her before the door closed and silence. 'You always were an early bird—still, I've got those figures you wanted to see ...'

Gerry spent the fifty minutes of her lunch hour in picking up a confusing array of literature, enthusing on the excellence of this washing machine or that. There was quite a selection for Teddy to choose from, though she rather thought she would favour the automatic. Crawford and William had been incarcerated in William's office all morning, and had barely looked up from the desk strewn with papers when she had taken their coffee in. Crawford had been too immersed to even notice her, she thought, when he hadn't looked up, and it had been William who had cleared a space for the two cups and saucers, remarking, 'You're a life-saver, Gerry.'

They had gone to lunch when she got back to the office, the door of William's room standing open. And when William returned without Crawford at half past two, she couldn't help the feeling of disappointment that flooded through her—though of course it was what she really wanted, she reminded herself again. The less she saw of Crawford the better. As the afternoon wore on, her nerves became stretched as each footstep in the corridor outside had her convinced that he was about to come through the door. At half past four she decided he must either be with some of the other top brass, or he had gone back to London. She refused to cogitate on what or who was so important in London that he had to go dashing back there.

Then all thoughts of Crawford were chased from her mind, for the phone rang, and it was Teddy on the line— a Teddy who sounded so fretful, so tearful, and so much the way she had been before Gerry had been ill that Gerry was overcome with remorse that she hadn't given her sister so much attention recently.

'Oh, Gerry!' Teddy wailed, and Gerry knew she was only just holding back the tears.

'What is it?' she asked urgently, thoughts of one of the twins upsetting boiling water over themselves flashing horrifically through her mind.

'I can't tell you over the phone.' Gerry relaxed slightly,

her initial panic easing up. 'You will be home early, won't you?' Teddy pleaded.

Gerry became aware that William had come out of his office. 'Yes, Ted—I'll be home on the dot of five-fifteen, I promise.'

The phone went dead at the other end. Teddy had become too upset to even say goodbye, Gerry thought distractedly, as she replaced the receiver and turned worried eyes to William.

'Trouble?' he asked kindly.

She didn't know if Crawford had told him anything of her home circumstances when he had told him she wasn't to work overtime, but at the sincere look of sympathy on his face she felt he would keep anything she told him to himself.

'I live with my sister—she feels a little insecure sometimes. I ...'

'She's having an attack of the ab-dabs now,' William said with such instant understanding, she rather thought Crawford must have given him an outline of her family circumstances. 'Why don't you nip off home now and keep her company?' he suggested. 'It's not long to go before five anyway—and what you're doing there can wait until morning.'

'Do you mind—I'll ...'

'I insist on it.'

Thoughts of William's kindness stayed with her as she hurried through the swing doors and into the street. Then thoughts of Teddy took over her whole attention. Teddy hadn't been the way she had been on the phone for ages—she'd been perfectly all right this morning, had taken Sarah's screaming in her stride and hadn't flapped at bit, which made Gerry wonder what had happened to cause her to take this step back.

Teddy was sobbing in earnest when she'd parked the car and hurried through the back door of the cottage, and with her protective instinct all to the fore, Gerry rushed to put her arms round her sister and tell her everything was all right.

But as Teddy began to tell her what had happened to cause her to be so upset, all the love and understanding Gerry was showering on her turned to amazement, then to dismay, disgust, and finally to downright anger that her sister could have been so uncaring of her feelings to have done what she had done.

CHAPTER TEN

'PAUL was here this afternoon,' Teddy sobbed, sitting on the settee with Gerry holding her hand soothingly. 'I haven't told you before, but there's been a sort of warmth growing between us. He's kissed me a couple of times and I couldn't help but respond.'

Gerry blocked out thoughts of the way she hadn't been able to help responding to Crawford. Teddy was the one with the problem—she needed all her concentration to try and help her with that, whatever it was.

'Anyway, like I said, he came this afternoon, and he kissed me again, and we talked and talked, and,' Teddy gave a sob and Gerry squeezed her hand sympathetically and waited until she had sufficient control to continue. 'I thought he was on the point of asking me to marry him, a-and I was getting ready to say yes—I know I shouldn't show I'm so eager, b-but I love him.' Teddy wiped her eyes, and Gerry thought that any minute now she would be crying herself. Then Teddy went on, 'Paul just beamed at me as if he already knew what my answer was going to be —then one of the twins woke up and spoiled the moment, and then Paul asked if I thought you would babysit to-morrow night as he had something to say that didn't bear interruptions ...'

'Yes—yes, of course I'll babysit,' Gerry inserted, won-dering if this was why Teddy was so upset. They didn't look to be tears of happiness somehow, but one never knew with Teddy.

'B-but I can't go ...' Teddy wailed. 'Not now ... Not after what Paul said ...'

'What did Paul say?' Gerry urged gently, while Teddy made a brave effort to control herself.

'Well, after I'd settled Emma, the romantic mood was broken, and I didn't want him to propose right then. I wanted his proposal to be something to remember— you know, candlelight, that sort of thing. When I came back to Paul he asked if I'd been happy with Mark, and one thing led to another, and he told me he'd almost married once, but that he found out the girl he was engaged to was two-timing him. She had another man friend, an older man. This girl was always dressed up to the minute and Paul never questioned how she could afford it, and then just before the wedding he found out this man paid for his fiancée's clothes—found out that this man had lent her no end of money.'

'So what happened?' Gerry asked, unable to see the re-levance to Teddy's relationship with Paul in what she was telling her, but knowing Teddy wouldn't feel better until she'd got it all out of her system.

'Paul threw her over—he said he could never marry a girl who took money from another man, could never marry a g-girl who owed another man money ...' Teddy's voice broke off into anguished sobs, so that Gerry began to fear for her, and almost missed hearing her sob, 'Paul will never m-marry me once he knows another m-man paid for the dress I'm wearing now.'

'Man?' Gerry echoed. Teddy was certinly mixed up.

Mark's great-aunt had paid for the clothes they were both wearing. 'What man, Ted? The money we spent on Saturday came from Mark's great-aunt, didn't it?'

Teddy didn't answer, and as she waited, Gerry forgot for the moment that her sister was breaking her heart in front of her—a sickening feeling of dread was growing inside her that Teddy had lied about Mark's aunt. 'Didn't it, Teddy?' she asked urgently, and when Teddy still made no reply, she did something she had never done before. She took hold of Teddy's two arms and shook her twice. 'Where did the money come from?' she asked firmly, and forced Teddy to look at her, knowing her sister wouldn't look her in the eyes and tell her a lie.

Teddy took a deep breath, then, her eyes filling with tears again, for the first time in her life feeling afraid of the set look on her sister's face, the brown eyes refusing to back down at her entreating look, she whispered, 'Crawford.' And as Gerry looked back at her as if unable to credit what she was hearing, she went on, 'Crawford Arrowsmith gave me five hundred pounds.'

Gerry felt she was going to faint with the shock of what Teddy had just told her. Unable to sit and look at her sister, she stood up, her hands dropping away from Teddy's arms, any sympathy she had had with her dissolving at the enormity of what Teddy had done.

'How could you, Teddy—how could you?' she accused, her mind trying to take in Teddy's words, while everything within her was screaming that it couldn't be true, that Teddy had made it all up—but knowing Teddy wasn't lying.

'It's all right for you,' Teddy came back, aggressive in defence. 'You don't mind how you look—but I wanted to look nice for Paul. I'm fed up with wearing rag-bag dresses. I'm fed up with never having any money for extras. When Crawford said I could have the money . . .'

'You didn't ask him for it?' Gerry's eyes flew to her sister.

'Of course I didn't,' Teddy snapped, her tears forgotten. 'We chatted often while you were ill, and I told him we were always broke, how we never had anything new.'

Gerry remembered Crawford's eyes on her only that morning when she had told him her outfit was new. My God, she thought, he must have known he had paid for it! She groaned aloud, and sank down on the settee again.

'What are we going to do, Gerry?' Teddy's eyes were moist again, begging her to find an answer to her problem.

'I don't know what you're going to do,' Gerry said slowly, for once in her life feeling completely unmoved by the sight of her twin in tears. 'But I'm going to see that money is paid back. How much have you got left?'

'I'll go and get it.' Teddy seemed in full agreement with the idea and sped upstairs, while a still stunned Gerry sat and looked blankly at the wall in front of her. She couldn't get over all the lies Teddy had told her, though able to understand how she felt about the hand-to-mouth existence they lived. But to actually take five hundred pounds from a stranger—from Crawford! Gerry blanked her mind off as Teddy came back into the room.

'There's three hundred and fifty pounds left.' Without saying a word Gerry took the money from her and placed it in her bag. 'What about the other hundred and fifty pounds, Gerry?' Teddy asked tentatively.

Gerry looked at her and read her mind accurately. She knew Teddy was breathing a heartfelt sigh of relief that she was prepared to take the debt over, and even when she wanted to remain angry with her for the position she had put her in, Teddy was her sister after all, and she had been through a very bad time.

'Don't worry about it, Ted,' she said, softening, unable to be angry with her for very long. 'What you tell Paul is your own business—but as of now you don't owe anybody anything.'

'Oh, Gerry. I'm a bitch, aren't I?'

Gerry could see Teddy was trying to look penitent, but it didn't quite come off—not with the sparkle that was beginning to creep back into her eyes. 'You are,' she agreed, thinking it not right that Teddy should get off too lightly. Then as the smile went from Teddy's eyes, 'But I'll still babysit for you tomorrow night. Now I'm going upstairs— I have some thinking to do.'

Gerry was upstairs for over half an hour, during which time her brain had thawed from the frozen numbness Teddy's revelations had dulled her into, to a determination that she meant every word of what she had said downstairs. Somehow Crawford Arrowsmith was going to take his money back.

It came to her that the day she had seen Crawford's car disappearing away up the hill must have been the day he had called to hand the money over to Teddy. All that talk about him calling to tell her the A35 was being delivered the next day had been a cover. Teddy already had the money in her possession the day she'd bought the T-shirts for the twins, and bought the lipsticks. Teddy would have to hold back with her story about Mark's great-aunt until she was back at work, she realised, because until then she would have been in the cottage when the post was delivered and would have known there was no letter.

Leaving the bedroom, Gerry went and washed her face and hands, and returned to apply a light smear of lipstick— pausing to bolster her defences when it came to her that not only had Crawford paid for the suit she was still wearing, but had almost certainly paid for the lipstick too. She saw no point in changing, and went downstairs.

'I'm going out for a while,' she told Teddy. 'I'm not sure how long I'll be.'

Teddy didn't ask where she was going; she wouldn't

need too many guesses anyway. 'I'll be all right now, Gerry—take as long as you need.'

Heading the A35 in the general direction of Layton, Gerry knew she had to have this matter settled tonight. She had to see Crawford and get it all over and done with—her nerves were stretched to breaking point, so that she had to exercise stiff control not to think of anyone or anything. To put Teddy and Paul, the future of Emma and Sarah out of her mind—for if Teddy and Paul were to marry, the future of the twins would be secure. But most of all she had to try not to think what Crawford's reaction would be when she found him.

She should have rung the office, she realised; he might be around there somewhere. She smiled a humourless smile as she drove along—here she was, determined to track Crawford down, and she didn't even know where he was! There would be no one at Arrowsmiths to tell her—even if they were ready to divulge his whereabouts. She didn't even know where William lived, and since he was more than likely ex-directory, there was no way of contacting him. But she knew where she was heading for, and that was the Creighton House, where William had told her Crawford always stayed. That he'd be staying there tonight was a long shot—but if he wasn't staying there, she was determined enough to invent some story to get his London address out of them. And if a journey to London proved necessary, well, so be it, she would go to London, and tonight.

Gerry was not conscious of feeling any emotion as she pulled up outside the discreet opulence of the Creighton House. All she felt inside was an ice-coldness. Up in the bedroom she shared with Teddy, she had got rid of all her remaining anger while she had reasoned that if Teddy married Paul, and she couldn't yet face thinking of not seeing Emma and Sarah every day, it naturally followed that Teddy would be moving out of the cottage. That being so, her own expenses would be halved and any money saved could be sent to Crawford each month until the hundred and fifty pounds was paid off. After that she would see about her own debt—the cost of the repairs to the A35, not to mention Mrs Chapman.

Leaving her car parked in the semi-circular drive, Gerry went into the thickly carpeted vestibule of Creighton House, her feet unerringly taking her to the reception area.

'I've come to see Mr Crawford Arrowsmith,' she said, forcing herself to sound confident while waiting for the girl to reply that he wasn't registered.

'I'm afraid he isn't in yet,' the girl said, her eyes checking over the rack holding several keys.

So he *was* coming back here tonight. Gerry masked her feelings of relief—she hadn't been looking forward to a journey to London. 'I'll call back,' she said, and went outside to sit in her car and decide what to do. Glancing at her watch, she saw the time was half past six, and felt she'd lived a month this past couple of hours. The receptionist had said Crawford wasn't in yet, which could only mean he hadn't left Arrowsmiths—that he was still working, unless he had gone to have dinner with William and his family.

Gerry contemplated what to do for the best, finally deciding she would have to sit it out and wait for him. For if he hadn't gone home with William, he might arrive at his hotel any minute, and it was on the cards he would have some evening engagement and would be going straight out again. No, safer to stay where she was rather than chance missing him.

She had less than ten minutes to wait before she saw the sleek saloon car she recognised swing round into the drive. She'd give him five minutes to settle in, she thought as his car swept past her with no sign of his having seen her, then she'd go in and get it all over with. She saw him get out of his car, and quelled the rising emotion within her that she would soon have to go in and pull no punches with the tall, aloof-looking man. Then, while she waited expecting him to go in the direction of the entrance, he turned, and without seeming to look at the A35 he began walking towards her, not stopping until he reached the window she had wound down.

'I'd like to see you if I may,' she said quietly, without giving him a chance to say anything. She knew her face was set—she didn't feel like smiling.

Crawford looked at her for a long moment, his own features unsmiling. Then like a second at some duelling match offering her a choice of weapons, he said coolly, 'Your car—my car—or my room?'

Since the idea of handing over the three hundred and fifty pounds in broad daylight where anyone passing might see did not appeal, Gerry said, 'Your room, please.'

If Crawford thought it must be serious for her to voluntarily offer to go with him to his room after the passion he knew could flare up between them, his face gave nothing of his thoughts away. He stood back, closing the door of her car when she was standing beside him. And without another word being said, he moved back the way he had come.

Gerry walked beside him, willing herself to stay calm. As Crawford collected his key, she managed a smile for the receptionist who remembered her from a short while ago. Then with Crawford's hand beneath her elbow, she went with him to the lift and stood silently beside him as they went up to his floor before going on to his room.

His room housed a bed and the usual bedroom furniture, plus a couple of easy chairs and a small table. The ceilings were high, she noted, and the room large and airy.

'Will you excuse me while I get some of the grime off,' Crawford asked, and shrugged off his jacket, which was followed by his tie, before he disappeared into the adjoining bathroom leaving the door open.

Gerry could hear the water running as he washed his hands. Nervous now—though she had no reason to be, she told herself stoutly—she clutched on to her bag that held the money that would shortly be in Crawford's possession. There was nothing at all to be nervous about—Crawford had been in error in the first place in giving Teddy the money; he would see that, surely?

A movement from the bathroom indicated that he was about to join her, and Gerry straightened her spine as she swallowed collected saliva in her mouth as the interview she wished was over was about to begin.

'Would you like a drink?' Crawford offered, coming into the room, and she noticed, quite irrationally she thought, since it had nothing to do with why she was here, how broad his shoulders were in the fine silk of his shirt.

'No, thank you.' She wished she'd put her hair up in a bun—that way she might have been able to collect some of the calm that was leaving her tenuous hold. Crawford was dominating this large room, and she had to be the one in charge of this interview. 'My business won't take long ...' she began.

'Business?' Crawford looked at her sharply, his eyes narrowing slightly, as though to say he preferred to conduct business at his place of work.

'You didn't suppose I came here on a—social call, did you?' That's right, get some aggression going, she thought. She felt better able to handle him when she wasn't feeling weak-kneed about him. Though that was a laugh; she doubted there was a woman breathing who could handle Crawford.

Crawford noted the aggression in her voice, she could tell from the way his nostrils flared briefly. She knew he didn't like it, but he didn't rise to it.

'I'm past *supposing* about anything you do, Geraldine,' he stated coolly, going on to tell her, 'I've known one or two women in my time,' and that, she thought, was an understatement, 'but never have I come across one who's so hellbent on self-destruction.'

'Oh?' She hadn't meant to voice that as a query. She wasn't here to debate what Crawford thought about her personally—why didn't she just hand over the money and go? Her hand moved to the clasp of her handbag, but that was as far as she got, for he was laying into her with no holds barred.

'You take the first prize any time for misguided feminine thinking! What you hope to achieve the way you go on I fail to see.' She had no need to ask if he was referring to the way of life she and Teddy led, it was crystal clear, as was the fact he thought she was making a very bad job of it. 'You take over your sister and her family without thinking twice about it, don't even stop to think about the demands made on you, take without hesitation on your own shoulders every crisis that turns up, and are too damned proud to think of asking anyone else for help.'

'Who would I ask for help?' Gerry found her voice, only to wish she could have delivered her question with less heat, for the whole time he had been slating her, his voice had been icy cold. 'You know it all,' she challenged, 'you tell me where I should turn to for help—even the man I was thinking of marrying didn't want to know!'

Crawford stilled for a moment as her words hit him, then tight-lipped he asked the question, 'Does that mean you're no longer thinking of marrying him?'

Gerry chose to ignore his question; it was none of his business anyway. Crawford turned away from her and helped himself from a bottle of Scotch on the side table, downing the contents of his glass in one swallow before turning back to her.

'Apart from our own welfare department—who I know would have been pleased to assist you—there are numerous organisations only too willing to give help and advice.'

His voice became hard. 'When I think of you two ...'

'We don't need anybody's charity,' Gerry broke in proudly, rising to her feet, her hand going inside her bag. 'And I didn't come here for a lecture,' she drew out the bundle of notes, 'I came to return some of the money you gave Teddy.' Her own lips were tight as Crawford ignored her outstretched hand. Since he made no attempt to take it from her, she dropped the bundle down on the table before her. 'There's three hundred and fifty pounds there—I'm afraid we'd spent some of the money before I knew where it had come from.'

Suddenly Crawford moved, and in a flash he was close up to her, his hands tight bands on her arms as he hauled her nearer, forcing her to look into fierce slate grey eyes that caused her to want to shrink back at the unchecked fury she saw there.

'You can't bear to take my money, can you?' he gritted harshly. 'It really sickens you that you've inadvertently spent some of my money. That you've actually lowered your pride, however unknowingly, to be standing up now in something I paid for.'

'Yes—yes, it does!' she fired back, stamping hard on the fear inside her that made her want to run from his anger. It didn't surprise her that he knew he had paid for her suit. 'Unfortunately, I've worn this now, so it can't be taken back to the shop—but the other dress I bought will be taken back the first chance I get.'

'*You bitch!*'

Gerry paled as he bit the word at her. If her slinging back his charity in his face had mortally wounded him, he couldn't have put more feeling into his utterance. His hands dropped away from her and he turned so she couldn't see his face, and she had a feeling he was as disgusted with himself as he was with her.

'I'm sorry,' she said quietly. 'But you must see that I cannot allow you to ... to finance Teddy and me.'

'Why not?' He had himself under control now, and his look when he turned was faintly mocking. 'Are you afraid I might ask you to repay the debt in kind?' Gerry's eyes widened at his words, and widened further as he came a step closer. 'Come to think of it, that's not such a bad idea.' Gerry retreated a step as he went on coolly, 'Let me see,' he paused as if calculating the outstanding amount. 'By my reckoning you still owe me a hundred and fifty. Seems a bit pricey, I must admit—but you're quite attractive in your way.'

She sensed then that somehow she had hurt him deeply, and that to frighten her was his way of salving that hurt, but she had no further time to analyse that thought, for Crawford's arms were coming towards her, and with a muttered, 'Why the hell not?' he had hauled her up against him and his head was blotting out the light. Then his mouth was over hers in a brutal, ruthless kiss, as if he was trying to assuage all the hurt that was in him.

Gerry struggled furiously against him as with cold deliberation, one hand just below the small of her back, he was pressing her to him, and she felt the hard lines of him against her as he forced her body to him.

'No,' was all she managed, when his lips left hers briefly. Then her lips were claimed again. She didn't want to be kissed by Crawford—not like this. He was deliberately trying to make her feel cheap. There was nothing tender in his kisses, and he was too strong for her female strength to fight for very long.

She felt his hands unbuttoning her waistcoat, felt the warmth of his touch against her and knew he had successfully unbuttoned her shirt too, as she felt the warmth of his hand against her skin. Then he was carrying her over to the bed, her furious struggles making no impression on him. She kicked and fought, but all to no avail—she felt her legs go from beneath her, felt briefly the softness of the mattress beneath her, then Crawford's weight was over her and his mouth was ravaging hers. Brutally he kissed her, his hands moving over her waist and upwards in investigating movements to come up to her naked shoulders.

How far he would have gone she had no idea, but she felt her strength giving out, and tears of regret that this would be the remembrance she would carry of the man she loved when it was all over sprang to her eyes and trickled down the sides of her face to stop their passage when they came into contact with Crawford's skin. For some moments he didn't appear to comprehend what the salty wetness was, so far had his anger against her overtaken him.

Then suddenly his weight was transferred from her, and he lay on his side, his look showing a different sort of pain she didn't recognise.

'Oh God, Gerry,' seemed to be dragged out of him, 'I've scared you half to death, haven't I?' Then as Gerry could only lie there as if turned to stone, her full brown eyes searching every plane of his face, her fear of him gone without her knowing why, other than that instinct was telling her he wouldn't attack her again, 'Forgive me, my dear, if you can,' he said softly, then almost reverently he placed a kiss of such exquisite sweetness on her mouth, it took every scrap of reserve she had left not to put her arms round him and hold him to her in the forgiveness he asked for.

She was in no way alarmed as she lay there, her breathing as ragged as his through the exertion of fighting him, when his hands came down to refasten the shirt and waistcoat he had so ruthlessly opened. Then he had left her and gone to stare out of the window.

Coming to her senses at last, Gerry scrambled off the bed, tucking her shirt into her skirt as she straightened up. What would have happened if Crawford hadn't felt the wetness of her tears against his skin, she didn't want to think, but now it was all at an end, and all she wanted to do was to go. To get out of this room and go somewhere where she could be alone for a while.

'I ... I know it's a sore point with you, Crawford,' she addressed his back, knowing everything had to be said now, even if it meant risking his repeated wrath, though she knew he wouldn't kiss her again. Once outside this room, she wanted never again to have to refer to the money. 'But I must tell you I shall be sending you a cheque each month until our debt is cleared.'

'There's no need.'

For him, she knew, it wouldn't matter. The amount she would send him each month would easily be swallowed up in petty cash—but it seemed to her that the last thing she could do for Teddy was to honour her debt and allow her to go to Paul with a clear conscience.

'There's every need.'

'Why?'

He didn't sound as though he was interested any more, and Gerry turned to the door ready to leave. She had to have the last word, and it had to be convincing, otherwise she could see he would rip her cheques up when they arrived on his desk every month.

'A bride doesn't like to go to her future husband owing a debt to another man,' she said, and began walking towards the door.

She didn't get very far. Unaware that Crawford had moved, she found him behind her, his hands coming to rest on her shoulders, not tightly, but firm enough to hold her.

'You're still in love with Preston—you're going to marry him?'

It took her a moment or two to catch up with his train of thought, then with her back still to him, 'I am not in love with Robin Preston—and I have no intention now or at any time of marrying him,' she said clearly, and felt herself being turned round so that he could see into her eyes that she was telling the truth.

'Then who the hell are you going to marry?'

'It's not me that's getting married—a-and Paul Meadows hasn't actually asked Teddy to marry him, but she thinks he's going to,' Gerry said quietly, hoping Teddy would forgive her for breaking her confidence, though not knowing quite what to make of the way Crawford was looking at her.

He seemed to meditate for a second or two, then right out of the blue he said something that shook her so completely, she said croakily:

'What did you say?'

'I said, Geraldine Barton, that since you're not otherwise committed, why not marry me?'

Gerry tried to stem the trembling that had started up inside her, and pulled herself out of his hold so he shouldn't be aware of how much his unexpected proposal had shattered her.

'I—er—you did say marry you?' She had to ask again, and was pinned by his look as he nodded in confirmation. She moistened her lips with the tip of her tongue. 'Er— why would you want to marry me?' she asked, trying to think of one good reason why he should, when all she could think of were a dozen good reasons why he should not. Then not waiting for him to speak, 'I know there's a —physical attraction between us,' she had to admit that much since he already knew he had the power to make her senses sing. 'I don't mean that ... that ... just now,' she added hastily. 'You terrified me then.' She saw a look pass over his face that told her he regretted his roughness with her.

'You mean the time we were out in the car and you called a halt before my experiment was finished?'

'Experiment?—— There didn't seem to be anything experimental about it from where I was sitting.'

'Oh, but there was.' Her look told him he could have fooled her. 'I never intended kissing you when we set out on that drive,' he told her. 'I thought it would give ...' he broke off without finishing. 'Well, never mind what I thought, but once I'd begun to kiss you—and I'll admit your response was most unexpected—I decided to find out just how far you would go, though you were never in any danger, for all you got so panicky.' Gerry felt her eyes caught and held by his slate grey look. She wanted to insert two or three questions at that point, but something was telling her to stay quiet. 'I thought that if you showed signs of being ready to go all the way,' his eyes flickered as he watched the blush stain her cheeks, 'then it would mean you were no longer in love with Preston. When you told me you didn't want to make love, I took it to mean you were in love with him. Now you tell me you're not in love with him, I'm left wondering if I've been wrong about a few other things as well.'

Gerry looked away from him then. She had no intention of revealing how much she loved him, and still couldn't think why he had suggested she marry him. But it seemed since he was going part way to being honest with her, the least she could do was to show him some honesty in return.

'I didn't want to stop you that day,' she admitted at last, feeling as though compelled. 'It was just that I didn't want —to be a—casual affair.'

'You mean you wanted a more permanent relationship?' Crawford said carefully.

His very words had her heart fluttering again within her. To say 'yes' to that would reveal too much, and she rather thought she had revealed too much already. Then Crawford was saying in the same careful tone, 'Marry me, Gerry— I promise you it will work out.' He still hadn't told her why he wanted her to marry him, and she knew she couldn't ask

—that was until it suddenly dawned on her he was feeling sorry for her.

'You feel sorry for me.' It was out before she could stop it, and at the questioning look on his face she was forced to carry on. 'You're thinking that with Teddy married to Paul I shall be lonely without her and the twins.' She would be, of course, as yet she hadn't faced up to the anguish she would feel when Teddy took Emma and Sarah with her, feeling as she did since she had nursed them since they had been tiny babies that they were as much hers as Teddy's.

'You won't have time to be lonely if you come to me,' Crawford told her levelly. Then putting it on the line that their marriage, if it ever happened, would be a true one in every sense of the word, 'You'll be too busy looking after our babies.'

Again colour suffused her cheeks. She could think of nothing she would like better than to have Crawford's babies, and she lowered her lids so he shouldn't see the hint of moisture there.

'What if Paul doesn't ask Teddy to marry him?' she asked, knowing she was talking herself out of being Crawford's wife, when it was something she wanted with her whole heart. 'What then?—— I wouldn't be able to leave Teddy to fend for herself.'

'If you do me the honour of marrying me, Gerry, then naturally your family will become my family. Teddy will have a house of her own, a nanny if she wishes, and as many staff as she thinks fit to run the house for her.'

Gerry clenched her hands at her sides at the goodness of this man. Unlike Robin who had refused even to discuss Teddy, let alone try and think up ways to help her—even though Crawford was in a vastly different financial bracket, he hadn't hesitated when the subject of Teddy came up.

'Oh, Crawford,' she said softly, and saw him standing stiffly a yard or so away from her, and had no idea why he was prepared to do all this for her. Then suddenly it came to her that she had been up in the clouds for the last five minutes ever to think of accepting his proposal. He was apparently prepared to give her everything she wanted except love, and loving him as she did, how could she possibly accept what he offered, having nothing to give in return.

'Does "Oh, Crawford" mean you accept my proposal?' he asked, sounding so stiff she couldn't at once answer him.

'No,' she said, and studied the carpet at her feet, and so missed the tightening of his jaw. 'I'm honoured that you've asked me to marry you but it wouldn't be right.'

'Why wouldn't it be right?'

Crawford's voice was conversational, giving no hint whether her refusal had pleased him or otherwise. Trust him to want everything put neatly in order before he filed it away, she couldn't help thinking, knowing her own pride had taken away from her the one chance of happiness she had. Crawford would go out of her life now, he would not repeat his proposal—even now it was growing cold between them.

She turned away from him and started towards the door the way she had done previously. This time he made no move to stop her, even though as yet she had not answered his question. A depressing weight of sadness enveloped her as she stood with her hand on the handle of the door. It seemed to her then that her life had been ruled by pride. Pride had ordained that no one outside the walls of Honeysuckle Cottage should know what a hard job it had been to make ends meet. Pride had ruled that she never showed any signs of weakness. And now with Crawford's proposal as dead as if it had never been uttered, pride had taken her one chance of happiness away. And suddenly she rebelled that pride ruled her life. What did it matter if the whole world knew she and Teddy were on their uppers? It hadn't bothered Teddy too much—she'd had no qualms in accepting Crawford's money. She had her hand on the door handle, when Crawford's voice, sounding oddly hoarse in her ears, came to her.

'Since you can't give me the courtesy of an honest answer, Gerry, would you hurry up and get out of my life?'

She turned at that and took two paces into the room, knowing she had done with pride, and saw a look on Crawford's face that had her going weak at the knees, for it seemed to her from that look that he was taking her refusal badly, and wanted her out of his sight quickly so that he could take recourse to the bottle or whatever form of solace he chose to take.

Discounting that look, she lifted her chin. 'You asked for an honest answer, Crawford—I'll give you one,' she said, knowing when she said it she was going to cry. 'I can't marry you because ...' even pride's fall didn't come easily, and she was forced to swallow it down before she brought out, '... because—I love you so much I ...'

'*What* did you say?'

The room was hushed as he stared at her as if unable to believe what he had heard. There was a tenseness about him that told her she had embarrassed him, but having sunk her pride so far, she wasn't going to back down now.

'I said I love you,' she said clearly. Then knowing he wouldn't want the further embarrassment of seeing her in tears again, she turned quickly, intending to get out of his room with all speed.

But as quick as she was, Crawford was at the door before her, blocking her way, a look on his face of incredulity —a look that said he didn't believe it, but since she had been foolish enough to tell him what she had, there was no way she was going to get out of the room until he'd heard more.

Then it was Gerry who was being unbelieving, for Crawford snatched her up in his arms, and she was too bemused to even struggle as he took her over to one of the easy chairs and sat down with her on his lap, holding her tightly to him as though suspecting she would at any moment take it into her head to fly away from him.

'Darling, darling girl,' he said tenderly. 'I never in a million years expected to hear those words coming from your lips to me.' And while she was still wondering at the gentleness his tone held for her, his head came down, and when his lips met hers, he successfully blotted out any further thought as she unreservedly returned his kisses.

It didn't matter to her then that he didn't love her—his kisses and caresses were so much what she needed at that moment. All the sadness within her was swept away as his mouth found her eyes, her ears, and traced kisses into the vee of her shirt. Unrestrained she clung to him, her very ardour proving she had not been lying when she had said she loved him.

Then after one long lingering kiss, when her lips had parted and she had clung to him as though she never wanted the kiss to break, Crawford put her away from him, cupping her chin with his hand, a light in his eyes that hadn't been there before.

'I said earlier you'd been in no danger from me the last time you responded to me,' he reminded her. 'I'm afraid, my love, I can no longer say with any conviction that that's now the case—so if you don't mind . . .'

Gerry had no idea what he had in mind—though anything would have been all right with her then. But to her regret when she would far rather have snuggled up close to him, he stood up with her in his arms, placed her back in the seat he had vacated, and went to take the chair facing her.

'You're beautiful, Gerry,' he said, looking across at her. 'Beautiful,' he murmured, 'even without that warm colour I can only assume comes from making love.'

She blushed hotly at that, and realised his teasing was an attempt to get some heat out of the moment. He made some comment to the effect that her blushes made him want to come over to her and kiss her again, but he didn't move, but stayed where he was.

'While I still have a little sanity left, I think we'd better arrange one or two details,' he said, giving her a warm look that had her on fire for him again. 'I want to marry you without any waiting, so I'll contact an aunt of mine who'll be pleased to have Teddy and the twins if your sister's arrangements aren't off the ground by then. Then we'll ...'

Gerry just had to stop him—he was going much too fast for her. She knew he wasn't in love with her, but even so there had to be some solid reason for him wanting to marry her other than the undoubted physical reaction they drew from each other. He had been watching her the whole time, and as a slight frown appeared on her brow, he leaned forward to ask urgently:

'What is it, Gerry? You are going to marry me, aren't you?'

'I ... I want to marry you, Crawford,' she said, after a faltering start, and saw him relax from his sudden tensing. 'And I've told you why—but—I have no idea why you want to marry me.'

Crawford looked at her as though he couldn't understand her question, then told her—which had the blood roaring in her ears, 'I thought you knew—I've loved you almost from the first. I've loved you from the time you looked at me in the chilly way you adopted and without knowing it, challenged me to do something about it.'

'Crawford!' His name escaped her, and all inhibitions forgotten, she was out of her chair and going to sit on the floor beside his chair, her hand resting on his knee as though she just had to touch him. 'I had no idea—you never said, looked, indicated or anything.'

'At the risk of living to regret this,' said Crawford, his hands coming down to settle beneath her armpits, 'come up here where I can kiss you.'

Once more at home in his arms, Gerry felt the warmth

of his kiss. It was gentle this time, as if he was making a
determined effort to hold back his passion. And as their
kiss broke, Gerry pondered on what she had said about
him not giving her any indication that he loved her—it had
been there all the time, but she'd been too blind to see it.
He had told her once when he'd thought Teddy was a
man that he had taken her home to see what sort of a man
would let her go about looking so ill. He had personally
taken her home from work instead of getting someone else
to do it. He had seen they had Mrs Chapman to lighten the
situation, and apart from giving Teddy the money which
enabled them all to have new clothes, she needn't look any
further than her spanking new A35 to know Crawford had
showed he cared.

'I'm going to make you happy,' she vowed, love for this
man holding her, threatening to drown her. Crawford kissed
her, and she forgot everything but the fact he loved her and
she meant all of what she'd said.

Then Crawford was setting her to her feet, telling her
she was headier than wine and suggesting that if they
didn't leave the confines of his room pretty soon, he
wouldn't be answerable for the consequences.

'Let's have dinner downstairs,' he suggested. 'Or do you
have to get back in a hurry?'

Not many men would have been so understanding about
Teddy, Gerry thought, especially at a moment like this. 'I
have all the time in the world, darling,' she said huskily.

Don't miss any of these exciting titles.

Complete and mail this coupon today!

Harlequin Reader Service

IN U.S.A.:
MPO Box 707, Niagara Falls, N.Y. 14302

IN CANADA:
649 Ontario St., Stratford, Ontario N5A 6W2

Please send me my FREE Harlequin Reader Service Catalogue.

Name _____

Address _____

City _____

State/Prov _____ Zip/Postal _____

ROM 2309

Don't let this chance pass you by!

And there's still *more* love in

Harlequin Presents...